MESSIAH

THE HORSEMAN'S TALE

RICHARD JACEY

First published in Great Britain as a softback original in 2022

Copyright © Richard Jacey

The moral right of this author has been asserted.

Design, typesetting and publishing by UK Book Publishing

www.ukbookpublishing.com

ISBN: 978-1-915338-19-8

Dedicated to the memory of the countless beasts of burden who suffered and died over the ages in peace and in war to serve the vain ambitions of mankind.

CHAPTER 1

V ery many years ago, in the lands at the top of the earth, there was a great kingdom. At night, the sun set behind tall, black mountains enamelled with snow, and rose again at dawn above deserts where nomads wandered eternally with their camels like driftwood across the sands. Between these two frontiers lay grassland plains so vast that no human spirit, gazing upon those wide horizons, could be otherwise than free.

The people who ruled in this secret land had come here many centuries ago, an army carried on the tide of some forgotten war and left, according to legend, by the great khan who led them, to found a city on the rim of his empire, while he went on to die in battle far from his birthplace. It was a legend that was rooted in truth.

They found this land very fit for horses, for horses are creatures that, like men, will seek horizons, albeit for different reasons. A horse looks to see what might come towards him, the further away the better, while a man wonders what might be beyond that magic line where the plain meets the sky.

There was good grazing through spring and summer, and sweet water from the rivers that ran down from the mountains. Autumn gave merciful warning of winter, when the snows came and wolf packs hunted like flickering shadows over the frozen wastes to pull down the horses whose time had come.

The men who bred the horses came, as we have said, as warriors, and warriors they remained. The tribesmen whom they displaced herded sheep and goats, but these men were not shepherds, and their slaves grew corn and maize and in the river valleys planted vines and fruit trees, for they were not farmers. They valued spices, but were never merchants, taking these things in tribute from the caravans whose route lay across the plains they now called their own. It came to be universally accepted that untold wealth in gold and precious stones lay in the stronghold of their kings.

Their ruler came to the throne not by birth or conquest, but through a curious form of selection that took place every ten years in times of plenty and less frequently in times of famine or conflict. He was, perforce, a man skilled in the arts of open war and secret violence, of diplomacy and betrayal. That he rode like a hero, hunted his own falcons and his own hounds was a matter of course. If he lived long enough, he came to be a friendless man, learning there is no more dangerous enemy than he who was once a friend.

At the time of which we speak, the king was called Parmenion, known now by custom as the Old King, being in the last year of his reign. His writ ran to the corners of his unruly land from his only city which men called Sirika, a place that lay at a junction of the trade routes across the steppe. His palace, approached up steep streets behind giant fortifications, was known as the House of the Winds, and the walls that protected it had never been taken.

Of the four great gates that gave entry to the city, only the ruins of one now remain. You will have seen countless photographs of the mighty stone archway where the graven horses rear up together above the portal, an iconic image equalled only by the Lion Gate at Mycenae. A few years ago, before the present conflict, the coach loads of tourists trudged up from the car park below the famous archaeological site and posed in the gateway before they passed on up the worn stone pavement to the palace.

There came a moonlit night in summer, the lands being at peace and the tribes quiet, when the sentries on this very gate, playing a game with smooth white pebbles on the rutted cobbles to while away the cold hours before dawn, saw a traveller approaching along the dusty road below. That he travelled at night was strange, that he travelled alone doubly so, and that he came on foot more curious still. At first, paying him little notice, they thought him a beggar, or some mendicant holy man, but as he neared the keep they saw how he loped up the slope, erect and purposeful, and how, after all, he had a companion, for by his side trotted a mighty hound, wolf-grey and terrible.

Now you must know that in that far-off time of which we speak, no man went abroad with a dog at heel. Noblemen kept their packs for sport, and lesser men chained famished brutes to guard their gates, but a hound must feed, and so presents a wayfarer with a constant concern. Certainly none of the men above the gate that night had ever seen or heard of a vagrant such as this.

The captain of the guard, who was called Cleitus, was standing before his squad with all the white pebbles but one gathered hastily away when, at his nod, the porter drew the bolts of the postern gate, and the traveller stepped within.

For a moment there was silence, save for the guttering of the torches in their cressets on the archway walls. The traveller leaned with grace but thankfully upon his long staff, and the hound couched beside him, tongue lolling from his fangs. Their deportment was that of honoured guests who had arrived a little late. The captain, who was a veteran of many wars, saw that he was studied with a dark-eyed, empty gaze, and he stiffened slightly.

"Who are you, coming here by night?" he said.

"My name is Cephan, whom men call the Horseman."

The voice was low, but it carried strangely around the walls.

"What business have you here, at this hour?"

"I seek an audience with the great king."

Behind the captain, one of his men hawked noisily and then spat upon the cobbles at the traveller's feet. The traveller turned to stare at this man, and the hound let his great jaws gape. The captain put his hand to the hilt of his sword and cursed under his breath. The guard's grip on his spear tightened.

"Get up to the palace," said Cleitus to the guard, "and tell my lord's steward that I sent you, to know if the king will see this Cephan the horseman. For he sits late in his hall."

And indeed, the light of many torches blazed in the dark heights where the House of the Winds stood far above them.

"And the rest of you," said Cleitus "back to your posts. Now!"

The traveller leaned once more on his staff, and by the red, unsteady light of the cresset on the wall behind him, the captain saw that his face was thin and dark, with a nose like a blade between cheekbones high and prominent, and a mouth set like a sprung trap. His complexion was dark, save where a livid scar ran down the right side of his jaw. His hair, gathered in the nape of his neck by a leather thong, was black but grizzled by age.

He wore, this traveller called Cephan, a long, heavy fleece cloak over his leather jerkin and his leggings, and his dusty boots. At his belt, convenient to the right hand, hung a dagger with an ivory hilt. He bore the captain's stare without flinching.

"Why do you come here, to the king?" asked Cleitus.

"I have come," Cephan replied "concerning his horse."

Now the king's stables were famous throughout the land, and his horses numbered in hundreds, but Cleitus, like any man in the kingdom, knew immediately what was the traveller's business with his lord.

For in those days horses were valued beyond gold, and women. And for good reason. Tidings from the border, news from foreign lands, could travel no more quickly than a fast horse. Cavalry, to be swiftly deployed and effective in battle in these war-worn times, must be well- mounted. Asses and camels bore burdens, as did slaves, but warriors and men of consequence rode horses bred with fine discrimination over generations, and so proclaimed their consequence to the humble and the meek.

And it was the great king himself who had overseen the breeding of this horse to which Cephan had referred. His sire had come from the Arab deserts, and his dam was a mighty black mare from the Fergana valley to the east, sold to the king for so much gold that the merchant who brought her hired a hundred men to convoy him home. They murdered him while he slept, and took the gold.

In the fullness of time the mare bore a colt which all agreed was the finest ever foaled. From his sire he inherited his fine limbs and his grace and his speed, and from his dam came his great strength and stature. He was neither black nor grey, as had been his sire, for his coat was of a dark red-gold hue. Blood red, and indeed, it is still said that the Fergana horses sweat blood when roused.

Born in the palace stables, and reared in the fertile valley below the city, his early years were uneventful save for one unfortunate accident. A goatherd, trekking with his charges to Sirika but forestalled by the gathering dark, had chivvied his animals into a convenient pen before he found shelter on the king's farm. He had not seen the colt and his mother, peacefully couched together in a far corner. It was daybreak when the grooms discovered the mare and her colt, exhausted and terrified, standing atremble while the goats stampeded about them.

After the colt was weaned, they tried to stable him with an old billy goat in the next stall, so that he might learn that the horned, devil-eyed creatures of his nightmare threatened him not at all, but this only made matters worse, and the effort was abandoned.

Should the king be told? The horse master's dilemma had him sleepless for many nights. If he did, he would be lucky to escape with a flogging. If he did not, and the horse bolted with his rider, probably the king himself, from any passing goat, then a flogging would be a small price to pay.

Days went by, and nothing was said, until silence seemed to be the only way. It was not, after all, as if the horse would ever be taken on campaign. More than likely, he would get foals where he had been born and never leave the shelter of the farm.

He grew big and strong, fed the best forage the plains could furnish. He had his own guard, and although these men were well rewarded they were not envied. For all knew what would become of them should they fail to keep safe the king's greatest treasure.

The price of failure was sudden death, coming in the night, brought by men armed with silent blades and garrotting cords.

The robbers were brave and resourceful men, and had planned their attack well. They had already bribed one of the grooms to lead the colt quietly from the stables and out under the gateway where he shied at the bodies of the guards and his nostrils flared at the smell of blood. They had fresh horses waiting in the shadows there, and after cutting the groom's throat they made for the nearest border, a day's ride distant.

All might have gone according to plan, but the colt, unused to being led from another horse, slackened his pace, became frightened and finally stood dead in his tracks. His captors tried to whip him forward, and he lashed out with a scream of rage, reared up and plunged free, and bolted into the night.

Of the six robbers, one had been killed in the skirmish at the gate, and two more died when the rest were turned at bay by the king's better mounted patrol, a league short of the border. The three taken alive were less fortunate. They suffered long, hideous deaths outside the city walls. The people heard their sobs and their screams for mercy for four nights before they fell silent.

All important to Parmenion was the recovery of his colt. He might be captured by travellers, or he might stray beyond, into the mountains where the tribes held sway, acknowledging no master. And so twenty squadrons were sent on patrol, and it was said that for three moons not a mouse moved on that border but the king knew of it. Men were sent to the mountain chieftains to tell of the treasure awaiting those who secured the horse's return, but of those who came back, none had heard a word of his existence.

And there was no sign, not so much as a hoof print, of the colt. It was hoped at first that he had not ventured far, being softly nurtured. Surely, when he is hungry, his courtiers told the great king, he would come back and be none the worse for his adventure. But the king looked out upon the summer plains from his palace ramparts and could see the verdant grasslands stretching to the horizon, and the glint of silver streams. And for all he was a great king, he was a horseman too. And horsemen, true horsemen, never forget how sweet is freedom to these creatures, that liberty is their only heaven, that no horse ever wandered the eternal pastures bearing still the mark of man.

And so the king sent out mounted scouts to the steppe and to the hills. Finally, as the summer turned to a brief autumn, the colt was found. Found, but not caught, for he was running with his mares in a long, lush river valley of which he knew every stone. He had fought for, and had won, his own territory, and in his horse way, he had found a home in the foothills of the mountains. The king rejoiced that the animal had at least been found, and he dispatched chosen men to recover the wayward child of his heart. He anticipated their return before the winter, when cold famine haunted a land that trembled at night with the cry of wolves. For he reasoned that his horse, so gently bred and reared, might have flourished in the halcyon days but would never survive such harsh conditions.

The chosen men returned. Without the colt. They had found him, they had tracked him, they had driven him twice into ravines from which only a goat could escape, only to watch him surmount the cliffs with an easy grace that left them wondering if he could fly. They had tried to course him with relays of horsemen until he dropped from exhaustion, but their horses were not fast enough, and he simply disappeared over the hills, so that by the time they had tracked him again, he was rested and ready once more to play. For, they told the great king, it was as if he gamed with them. There was never a sign of panic, or even effort on his part. He would watch them come so far, and then he would forsake his mares and - here the tellers of this sorry tale spread their hands silently, unable to explain how this mortal horse had taken on such magical powers.

Of course they had tried, and succeeded, in corralling some of his mares, to trap him with. It had been difficult, for there was little timber, but they had set fires at the end of the ravine to frighten them, used what ropes they had, and set a patient watch against the horse's return. And return indeed he did. In the dead of night, coming down on them like a vengeful fury, screaming for his mares, heedless of the fires and breaking the ropes as if they were silken threads set by girls. The men had watched helplessly as he drove his harem to freedom. He was, they said, like no horse ever foaled. He was as mighty as he was beautiful, as imperious as he was intelligent. He possessed speed and endurance in equal measure beyond any they had ever seen, and he could go for days without water. In short, the great king their master, to whom they falteringly offered this explanation for their failure, had bred a horse that was truly come from a fable.

The king listened, sitting in his hall with his court about him, and his face never changed, nor did he utter a word of sorrow. But the sorrows of kings are never private, and all men knew why an old king might grieve for such a horse.

Winter came, and the steppe became a wasteland. The streams froze over, and there was grazing only for the wild ponies and the goats. The king kept his state in his fortress, and sometimes he walked the walls at night alone, and looked out upon a wasteland like sour milk under dead-white stars while the wolves paid tribute to the moon, and he thought of his blood-gold horse.

And when the spring came again, messengers brought him scraps of news, intelligence so scanty as to be worse than no news at all. There was a sighting of a stallion like no other in size and strength to the west of the kingdom, where the Tartars were, and another from the east, a second hand story from the desert. The king sent out his chosen men once more, and yet again they returned empty-handed.. The young men of his court, hungry for renown and royal favour, mounted searches into dangerous territories from which some did not return, and those who did bore only tales gleaned from nomads and the merchants in the caravans, of a mighty red horse, fearless of men, that ventured close to their tents and their camps but would not take water from the wells or eat the drugged maize left for him.

So now, with early summer flushing the steppe green again, the streams running free, and the nights tranquil with stars, we return to the postern gate where Cleitus waited with the traveller and his wolf-grey hound until his messenger returned with the royal command. Cleitus was to take the man up to the palace. The king trusted that if his well-regarded captain offered a bone, there would be meat on it.

The way to the House of the Winds was a steep avenue, paved by smooth, ancient stones. Cleitus led the way, and behind him in silence came the traveller and his companion, the two so close that they never in that journey made two shadows.

At the massive double doors of the king's hall waited his steward, a creature of silks and scent, who looked upon the party disdainfully as they advanced.

"You may follow me," he said, then glanced at the traveller's familiar,

"That animal must not go further."

"You may prevent him," the animal's master said calmly, "if you can."

Cleitus showed his yellow teeth between his bearded lips.

The steward turned to him.

"You must deal with this brute," he said with a sniff, "or His Majesty will know of it."

"Arselicker!" he replied. Cleitus was no lover of courtiers.

Then the doors were drawn open by the sentinels posted there, and the steward flounced forward into the king's hall, at that time a place of legendary splendour. Behind him stepped the traveller.

To either side, in ranks at their boards, sat perhaps two hundred men. For the most part, they wore the leather tunics and fleeces common in those lands, but here and there sat a group of men attired all in black. Bearded faces shone ruddy in the glimmering of the rush lights before them. They were noisy in drink and merriment, and from board to board moved young lads bearing flagons of the fermented mare's milk these warriors favoured. There was not a woman or a girl in the place.

Beyond them, high on a dais that faced the doors, sat the old, grey king, flanked by his courtiers with his son at his right hand, and here that black raiment was much in evidence. The entire hall fell silent as all eyes turned to the newcomers. A page came running down the aisle as fast as his thin shanks could carry him.

"My Lord bids you drink a cup with him." he piped, looking nervously up at Cleitus.

Now Cleitus and the king were bound by a bond that was more enduring than a lover's knot, more profound than the love of a father for his son, and sweeter than any sibling's tie. For years ago, when both were young men, they had been comrades in arms, and there had been a skirmish on the border in which, caught in an enemy ambush, Cleitus had saved the king's life. Then, he had been but one of many princes, but the fall of fortune's cards had made the boy a king, and Cleitus had grown old in his service until he had accepted his final post as captain of the king's gate.

Which is why Cleitus is now sitting with his king, who listens to him, and once is seen to smile, and sends the page running once more.

The traveller advanced in his turn, alone, up that aisle between the guttering rush lights that seemed ashamed to discover the congregation that sat there staring. Behind him went his familiar, his eyes never leaving his master's back.

The king looked down at the traveller,

"I am told you come concerning a horse that was stolen from me."

The traveller bowed his head.

"Indeed, great king." he answered, "I will bring him back to you."

He spoke calmly, but his voice carried throughout the listening hall, and there was a stir of expectation.

"You come on foot," the king said, "And you come alone."

"Your colt will not spurn me," the traveller replied, "because I come on foot, and alone."

The king had drunk deep that night, for he sought to dull the pain of a bad toothache with wine.

"It is a horse," he grunted at the man who stood erect and impassive below him, "not a wench for the wooing!"

On either side his courtiers stared and tittered. Cleitus watched quietly.

"I am not favoured for the love of women," said the traveller, "but your colt minds not such matters. Or you might have sent your noble son to bring him home."

He gestured to the lad who sat beside the king, a handsome youth who glowered as he drank from his goblet. The courtiers gasped almost inaudibly, but in the hall the men rocked in their noisy mirth. For the prince, as was well-known, had told his father that he was no herdsman, to be sent to find a missing horse.

"He couldn't bring home the goats, my friend!" yelled one.

The king sat in silence, waiting for the laughter to subside. He noted how long it eddied about the hall, and saw that his son was not respected by these men. The thought made him bitter.

"So I am to send a beggar!"

"A beggar is but a small charge." the traveller said.

"And his mules? And his escort?" Parmenion growled, "I can find better uses for my men and my mules."

"I need no escort," replied the traveller, "for I have nothing worth the taking - - -."

"Save a good mule!"

"An old one will suffer my lighter load, if he be sound."

Parmenion considered this.

"And what do you seek of me besides, if you bring back my colt?"

The traveller bowed low, but with dignity.

"Your favour, lord." he answered simply.

Parmenion shrugged wearily.

"An old mule for a hopeless cause."

"One thing more I need." the traveller said.

The king smiled.

"A sorcerer!"

It was a feeble jest, but the humour of a tyrant is best appreciated, and the courtiers tittered dutifully.

"In my Lord's mews there sits a falcon, a bird trapped but three days since. I wish to take her with me."

They stared, all of them, the steward and the courtiers, the pages and the servants, and the gathering of the chosen men who had edged from their places with a scrape of benches and a shoving for position so they could hear the exchange. So strange was the request that only Cleitus thought to wonder how the traveller came to know that the king's falconer had taken such a bird.

A page fetched this man, who on his knees confirmed the truth of what the traveller said.

The king's eyes, grey and baleful, stared down once more upon the vagabond before him.

"So you want the falcon to search for the colt?"

The traveller nodded briefly. Deep in the smoky hall, someone mistook the king's words, thinking he was jesting once more, and laughed. The tyrant's gaze traversed the benches and discovered the culprit who gave a curious gargle, as if his throat had been cut, and fell silent. Now sure that he had a madman in front of him, the king was at a loss. All holy books bespeak mercy for lunatics, and some say they are favoured by the gods. But this lunatic had teased him with an impossible fantasy, in his own court and before his chosen men.

At his elbow, Cleitus muttered something. The king gestured impatiently.

"Fetch me this falcon!"

And so the bird was brought before him, hooded, her talons fast on the falconer's leather gauntlet.

Now in those days all great men had their falcons and their hawks, and our king was a great man indeed. He had flown eagles since boyhood, and he looked now appraisingly at the mighty, lead-grey gyr-falcon that sat squat on the falconer's fist with her hooded head sunk between her wings.

"A fine bird," said the king, "and I have lost many of late."

"She is mine," the traveller replied "I took her from a nest two years since, in the snow country many leagues north of your Majesty's lands."

The king's frown cleared.

"Well then," he said, "let us see if she will come to her master's call!"

The courtiers smiled, and the warriors hooted their mirth, and banged the boards with their hands.

For as you will know, there is no link so fragile as that between a falconer and his bird. Save when she is hungry it barely exists at all, for she is governed only by her senses, and can have no thought of obedience.

"Set her free." the traveller replied.

The falconer turned to his master.

"She was full-fed not long since, Lord," he said doubtfully.

The king looked mockingly down.

"The dice fall against you!"

"Set her free." said the traveller once more.

The king stared. In the hall not a man stirred. Then he nodded, a slight but sufficient nod.

The falconer loosed the leather jesses, and flipped off the hood. And the falcon's head twisted about, her wings lifted like the wings of an angel, and she rose from his wrist steeply into the gloom of the high, timbered roof, and perched on a rafter, the better to survey the company below her.

The company below her looked up, saw how she seemed afraid, and then looked toward the traveller where he stood, impassively, with his great, gaunt hound at his side. These were children of the steppe, men who knew falcons as they knew horses, who saw immediately how knife-blade thin was the chance on which the man had gambled. Only Cleitus, watching not the falcon but the traveller's stony face, was prepared for what happened next.

The traveller pursed his lips, as if he whistled, but there was not a sound heard, save that up in the rafters the falcon screamed harshly and raised her wings, her ghost-grey wings. And then, when he raised his left arm, down she came, dropping so tenderly upon his wrist, her long talons hooking gently on his flesh, as if she cared not to hurt him. She folded those terrible wings across her dark back, and settled against his breast as if she had come home, and she mewed, as a falcon will, very rarely, when she is content.

"She comes," the traveller said, "to her master's call."

In the hall there was a murmur of astonishment, that faded to a silence as all waited on the judgment of the king.

Then Parmenion made a slight, impatient gesture of one gold-heavy hand.

"Let him take her," he ordered, "and a mule, and whatever else he requires."

Cleitus muttered again.

"And," the king continued in a voice that all could hear, "he has safe conduct in all Sirika, and may go where he pleases."

The traveller bowed, and turned back down the hall, between the ranks of onlookers, with one hand on the collar of his hound and the still-unhooded falcon on his naked fist. And to Parmenion's heart there came hope, a fanciful ghost of hope.

The ruins of that hall, where Parmenion held his state and the traveller came that night so long ago, can still be seen.

Tourists from all over the world used to trudge up the worn flagstones that make the way between the low, uncovered foundations of the houses that once stood there, and come to the stone entrance where the king's steward had his frosty exchange with Cleitus. Their words, and so many others, are echoes in that space. Some of the stone pillars that once supported the rafters where Phaedra took refuge still stand and some now lie in the warm sand. The mosaic that was the floor where Cephan stood and raised his fist and called her down to him, still remains. Only a few years ago, if you had successfully outwitted or bribed the marauding freedom fighters on the road from the modern city, you could see the blackened stones of the hearth where the logs blazed against the chill of that spring night. And you could hire a guide to show you about the fabled palace. He would tell you how it came to stand on that crag above the plain, and who were the men who ruled from that very stronghold. But if you asked what became of them, how Sirika fell, they would spread their hands and say, "It is not known."

When I first came to Sirika, there were not so many visitors. I drove unhindered from the modern city and parked close to the great gate. The stone horses reared above the entrance, the legacy of the men who made a great citadel and then, mysteriously, left it to stand undefended against the centuries, as it does today. I had arrived in the heat of the day, and found myself alone in the stony dust in the shade beneath the entrance. There, pausing to wipe my sweaty face, my eye fell on a small, smooth white pebble, so clean and shiny that it seemed to have some undiscovered purpose. So much so, that after a furtive glance about me, I put it in my pocket.

It is close by me now, where I sit beside the window to set down this strange history, and bring to an end many years of speculation and learned debate, in telling how it was that a man and a horse led to the fall of a great city.

CHAPTER 2

The king retired soon afterwards to his chamber, for his toothache troubled him still. Cleitus, alerted by a discreet page, joined him by way of a private passage and took the second couch, awkwardly as always, before the brazier. Julia, the old wolfhound, thumped her tail at him and lowered her grey head to her paws.

"No word of the emperor's man," said Parmenion as a sinister dwarf came silently forward with a flagon of wine.

"There is yet snow in the passes" Cleitus replied, and the king grunted morosely.

"He was here last year, while there was still snow."

"He will come" said Cleitus, "His master's cavalry suffer great losses on his borders, and he needs horses."

Parmenion sighed.

"Or he knows that the colt runs free, and has sent men to trap him."

He brooded on this for a moment, watching Cleitus stoop to take his cup from the dwarf's bird-like claw.

"They will make short work of our beggar if they meet him."

"You can abide the loss of an old mule, Sir!"

"I should not have sold those mares to that man!" the king muttered, staring at the coals in the brazier.

You did well enough in the bargain, thought Cleitus, but he did not say so.

The man of whom the king was speaking, the emperor's envoy, is known to history as Zhang Qian. The Han emperor who then ruled the vast and mysterious land to the east had sought to protect his long, mountainous border against the barbarians who threatened him from the west, with a great wall. He had garrisons stationed along its length, but the distances were too long for foot patrols, and so he needed horses. Fast horses, not the sturdy ponies upon which his cavalry rode to battle.

Now it happened that Zhang Qian, then a young courtier and a rising man, had been sent to seek an alliance with one of the border tribes. He had been held captive for his pains, and had been lucky to escape with his life. Lost in that uncharted wilderness that is now Uzbekistan, he had found himself in the Fergana valley.

And there he had discovered the horses of that place. A breed apart, known in ancient times as the heavenly horses, they were bigger, and more powerful, than any he had ever seen. Beautiful to behold and finely bred, their blood coursed so close to the skin that in exercise it took on a curiously rosy sheen. They were known to the horsemen of those parts as the "sweat-blood" horses. Their descendants still are.

Also, they had another, more valuable property. They could go for days without water. And a cavalry leader's constant concern is, where he might water the horses.

Zhang Qian had returned with the news of his discovery to the emperor, who had promptly sent him out on another journey, this time with a greater escort, to bring back as many of these prized animals as he could find.

His search had led him to Sirika two years earlier, in the early summer, when Parmenion's mares had their foals at foot. He brought with him for barter not gold but silk, bolts upon bolts of the cloth that seemed to be polished by any light that fell upon it, so fine and soft that it weighed almost nothing to the wearer. The fabled silk of the emperor's far dominions, made in his lands only, where the dread of his awesome power alone could keep safe the secret of its making.

And so the bargain was struck. Fine mares for fine silks. But no colts.

Parmenion remembered how he had showed off his stable to the envoy, proudly, as any horseman will, and had paraded the yearling chestnut horse, already a magnificent animal that seemed to disdain the earth he trod on. Somehow Parmenion had been uneasy then, without quite knowing why.

He discovered the reason the following year, when Zhang Qian returned, this time with a more powerful escort, and a mule train burdened with silk. He also had a silken gown, a shimmering blue robe, a present from the emperor himself – to a brother monarch.

The envoy's manner was infinitely courteous, but when Parmenion refused to sell the colt, despite the gift, Zhang Qian looked at him for a moment with his grape-like eyes, and then bowed over his folded arms.

"Perhaps my master will persuade you" he said quietly, "where I have failed."

In the evening of the next day the traveller left Sirika, leading an old mule that hardly protested when the falcon was perched upon its back, hooded now and tethered by a leash to the pommel of the pack saddle he carried. They made a strange group as they departed over the steppe, finally lost in its long shadows, the tall, gaunt figure of the man and his hound, and the mule with his unlikely passenger as still as a miniature sphinx. They marched in silence toward the North Star until the night was well advanced, and then made a halt, to spy followers. There were none, and at last the traveller made his camp by a stream. He hobbled the mule and turned him free, then put the pack saddle down beside his new-born fire. The falcon sat on the heavy wooden pommel with one foot peacefully raised into the pale plumage of her breast. The hound made a patrolling cast about the camp before he returned to throw himself beside his master who squatted to warm his hands at the blaze.

"A hard road, and a game we might have lost." said the hound, whose name was Khan, as he stared at the fire, "and all for you, faithless one."

Though the traveller knew that only the cold stars might hear, nonetheless he looked about him into the dark shadows. The falcon, whose name was Phaedra, roused her feathers, and the traveller plucked off her hood so that she might see her accuser.

"I am not of your kind," she said, "I give no word, betray no trust. I am as the wind in the sky, and I come to no man's hand unless it be my pleasure."

"Pleasure enough," said Khan with a sniff, "when you saw my master in yonder hall."

"So I came down to him. What would you do, cast up in such a company as that?"

Phaedra drew one of her wing feathers calmly between her mandibles.

"I had waited long enough," she continued, "since I was caught in that villainous trap. Men had baited it with a pigeon, and had broken its wings so that it struggled the more."

Khan sniffed.

"You were flown at a mountain hare."

"And I hunted him well, before I lost him in a thicket far away. Then I saw the pigeon."

"And then you thought only of your crop."

"I hungered, and hunger makes me weak, and in that state I cannot kill, and so I die! I hunt the skies alone and have no master. This man who starved me to some shift of an alliance, I favour more than any other. But Khan, I am not of your kind."

She roused her plumage once more, and sank her assassin head between those mighty wings.

"But we came a long road to recover you," Khan replied "He and I."

The traveller, listening silently to this exchange, smiled and cast a few sticks on his fire. The steppe is not rich in timber, and the store he had been able to gather was small.

"Not at her bidding, Khan," he said reprovingly, "Phaedra asks nothing of me. Rather I ask of her, and sometimes she is kind, and can help me. That is all."

Khan's grey head sank between his paws and Phaedra put her head under her wing, and seemed to fall asleep.

"If she had not come down to you" Khan said, "the king would have ordered you taken, and we would be his prisoners now."

"Indeed. But come to me she did, and so we have her with us now."

"What pleases you delights me also," the hound said, "but why?"

"I go in search of the king's colt, and I need her help. And I cherish her with all my heart."

"As you do me?"

"Nay, Khan," said the traveller very softly, and he pulled at one of the hound's ragged,rough-haired ears, "not as I care for you."

"Other men care for their women and their children." he continued, speaking as much to himself as to the great beast that lay beside him, staring into the fire, "and I care for the creatures I have found or they that have come to me, as you did. Phaedra I took from the nest, a bag of downy feathers that mewed like a kitten and fought as best as she could. I reared her, and manned her to me, so that she welcomed me when I came to her and mistrusted me no more. And so there arises a harmony, a secret pleasure in her company that warms my soul."

Phaedra, her head still under her wing, seemed to hear none of this, but in fact she heard it all. What credence she gave to his words, we cannot say.

Khan sighed in disapproval, then continued to look into the red embers with his yellow, wolf gaze as if he searched for his dreams there, like all his kind. The traveller fell silent, but his thoughts became words in his heart.

"She came into her glory when she was hard-penned, and her plumage was set. I saw a snow-maid awaiting her prince, and when she spread her broad, white wings and rose from my fist, it was as if she carried my sins with her into the cold air, and left them petrified forever."

Now they slept, Phaedra on her make-shift block, and Khan as close to the fire as he could creep, and both of them in some wise alert notwithstanding. The traveller stretched his limbs, and went to check the mule, then returned to his camp. All about him was the night, and stars strewn like the careless bounty of a spendthrift god, about to fall upon him.

It is time to learn a little more about this man we have called the traveller, and who called himself Cephan the horseman, and little it must be, for there were no records made of his passage into the world, nor of any of his doings in the forty or so years he had trod roads far beyond Sirika. But we know that he was palace-reared in the lands lying between the Tigris and the Euphrates, the son of a prince's favourite concubine, and that he showed early a curious affinity for horses. In boyhood, he haunted the royal stables, and as a youth his ability as a rider became a matter of pride to his royal father, and he was indulged accordingly.

As was common in those times, the father died by poison, and his harem was strangled by the eldest son, who rightly judged that his brothers in any degree must be murdered also. But our traveller escaped the search of the palace, being familiar with every passageway of the labyrinthine stables where he had spent the happiest hours of his boyhood.

And so, at the age of about twenty he was an outcast, lucky to have departed his homeland with the clothes on his back. He became a mercenary.

He fought for the Great King, and he fought against him, and he fought under any banner and for any cause or quarrel in the lands north and south of that tyrant's domain. He fought in Tartary, and he fought against the Bedouin of the Arabian sands. He escorted merchants in caravans, and with them he journeyed far into the east.

It follows from this, as the reader will understand, that he was a wanderer, a man of camps and garrisons, tents and bivouacs. Once, in Samarkand, he loved a girl, but she perished in childbirth, by which time he was fighting near Aleppo. A fine boy was born, but we do not know whether our traveller ever knew of him. There were other women, of course, but none of consequence, and by the time we come to meet him, our traveller was not much troubled by such needs.

He was a frugal man, as his way of life had dictated, and was as slim now as he had been in youth. He had been fortunate in his wars, for although disfigured by the jagged, livid mark on his cheek, and by other scars hidden by his costume, he had not been maimed, and could yet march his march if need be. That he was a peerless rider the reader knows, and that his strange affinity for horses had extended to his wolf-like companion. How he came by Khan is yet to be discovered, though we know already how he had taken Phaedra from her nest.

But our traveller had seen such things done in war, and even in peace, as sicken a man in his soul, and troubled by sins easily excused when he was young, he had wearied of his bloody career. For a man may carry his allotted weight of nightmare memories, and tuck them away in the crannies of his mind, but by and by they will trouble his dreams, and haunt even his waking hours.

He had found sanctuary, or so he thought, in the palace of a prince who ruled at that time, finding favour as master of the royal stables and keeper of the royal mews, and he had his own quarters, comfortable enough for any man and soft living indeed for him. He could not agree, however, with the grooms, the falconers, or any of the prince's household from the kitchens to the palace guard. They all complained loudly about his sudden bouts of violence and the days when he never left his bed. A woman, who might not have been lying, said she had been raped. The prince's chamberlain attempted to scold him, but the traveller beat the man with his own staff of office. He hardly seemed to notice the silence that fell on his appearance in the stables. He simply gave his orders and saw them carried out. But he did notice when one of the grooms spilled a water skin over his foot and then muttered only a word of apology. The man's miscalculation was a fatal one, as he knew in the moment before he died.

The prince bade farewell to his servant with real sorrow, but the traveller feigned his grief out of respect for an old man who had treated him with kindness. He knew that the abodes of men were no longer places where he could rest. The walls were always too close, the roof too low, the door so easily closed.

We discover Cephan again, squatting cross-legged over his dying fire, wrapped in his heavy coat, with Khan's muzzle on his lap, thinking of what the future might hold. Always he would be treated with suspicion, always his sinister mien would provoke a quarrel, always he would find himself a renegade once more. He had not known a mother since his early days, never a family, and not often friends. In his youth he had had comrades in arms, but now there was not a man on earth who would care whether he lived or died.

Staring now into the embers, he thought how he hoped to end his days. Perhaps a small house, with a tree in the yard for shade and a vine, well- watered and bearing a good grape - - - . if he could but gain the favour of this king.

Wrapped in his cloak, the traveller slept while the fire turned to cold, grey ashes, and Khan kept watch.

The dawn light revealed Phaedra, her head under her wing, her plumage roused up against the chill, sitting one-legged on the pommel of the pack saddle with the other drawn up into her breast feathers. Khan stretched and yawned. The traveller splashed water from the stream onto his bearded face and returned with the mule. He took Phaedra on his fist.

"I wish," he said to her, "that you would find for me the great king's horse."

Phaedra extended one wing, fanned out every long pinion like a lethal pack of cards, and looked at the traveller and Khan with composure. She made no reply.

The traveller repeated his request, and this time she scanned the eastern horizon, where the dawn opened like a mighty, pearl-grey oyster to display the rising sun. Still she said nothing.

Again and then again the traveller spoke, always softly and unhurried. He knew that she dictated the course of the exchange, that there might, indeed, be no exchange at all. Finally she scratched the back of her head with one talon.

"I look to kill before the sun sinks again."

"Aye," the traveller said, "but having killed - - -."

"I must rest with a full crop."

"I doubt it not," replied the traveller, "but then, it might please you to return to me. And if, perchance, on the plain below your wings you spy the horse, which is a red horse, as all men say -----."

"I know about the horse," she said, folding her wing so that it hung like a dark-bladed scimitar on her flank, "Not a falcon flies that has not seen him harried by men from the mountains to the plain. And now you would join the chase alone!"

"Not alone." Khan said.

"With - " She looked down at him with her yellow stare, "your – dog."

"Peace, Khan!"

Once order was restored, and the mule safely picketed, and Khan sulked off hunting, the traveller addressed his falcon again.

"I came to seek you, even in the court of the great king, when you were trapped," he murmured as winningly as he knew how.

Phaedra regarded him with contempt.

"I may discover the horse," she said finally, "and the wind may bring me back to you. But I make you no promise, give you no word of comfort. Wait for me if you will."

That yearning for absolute liberty, satisfied only when the sky reeled about her and the earth turned below, in a sudden took her, and she sprang from the traveller's fist.

Her white wings opened high, swept low across his face, and she was gone.

He could see now, by the early morning light, that his resting place was a good one. About the spring were trees, and some pasture for the mule. He found fuel enough for a few days' fires and saw how he might build a scanty shelter against the low, granite boulders from which the water welled. The sun was gaining strength, and warmed his face. Khan returned with a bloody muzzle, having killed a hare.

Our traveller broke his fast with a crust of unleavened bread and heated water to make a thin, green infusion of leaves that he had in a leather pouch. All about him the steppe marched away to the horizons. Where the sun was rising, he knew, there was desert, and in the west he could see, meandering through the grassland, the track he travelled and, far away, the mountains.

"What now, Master?" Khan said, lying at his feet.

"We wait."

"For the faithless one! But indeed thou art wise, and knowest all."

The traveller smiled at him, and shook his tangled, black locks.

"I know not what befalls us. It may be, that the gods have sent me here to die."

The hound shifted uncomfortably. He had heard his master speak of death many times, but he did not understand the word. That it betokened some great and mysterious event he could divine, listening to the manner of his master's speech and watching his countenance. And he could smell the fear that came with this word, and in his canine way he pitied his master, who was afflicted by it. He laid his great head on his master's knees.

"We wait," the traveller continued, "upon the flight of a falcon. If she returns, if she can guide me, then we will go search for the great king's horse. If she comes not, Khan, then I have no other road to follow, and this camp will serve my body for a resting place."

Through all that day they waited, and the next, often so immobile by the rocks that from a distance they might have been two of them. Sunlight splashed down through the trees and was wrinkled by the waters of the stream. The hobbled mule moved slowly as he grazed, or was still by hours.

The black silk night was sewn heavy with stars, a net, our traveller thought as he lay sleeplessly, to gather up his soul. In childhood, from the palace roof, he had wondered at them while in his nurse's arms, and now they were wonderful again. Perhaps, he mused, it is how the beginning meets the end at last.

CHAPTER 3

On the third day, in the evening, Phaedra came, spreading her wings to slow her descent to the rock in the shade of which Cephan lay, and then folding them precisely over her back. She hopped to the pack saddle on the ground at his feet, and Khan rumbled at her in his throat. The falcon had killed and eaten not long since, for Cephan could see that the plumage below her throat was ruffled by her stuffed crop. She blinked at him with her yellow eyes, and he feared she would put her head under her wing and fall asleep.

"We welcome you, Phaedra," he said.

She cleaned one of her talons with the murderous hook of her beak.

"You are fortunate indeed," she replied, "for I came down the wind and it carried me here."

"We are grateful to yonder wind," said Cephan humbly, "both Khan and I."

Khan stared pointedly away, and Phaedra roused her feathers and put up one dreadful foot into her breast, the four black talons hanging delicately together. There was silence for some time. Cephan roused himself to fan the warm ashes in his hearth, tended the fire to a paltry blaze, and saw that in the shadows the mule stood immobile in sleep. He could hear the chill, chaste meditation of the stream in the darkness beyond the firelight. Finally the falcon spoke.

"He is clever, your horse. He has found a valley in the foothills of the mountains, made secret by the lay of the land, and there he keeps his mares. There is water and grassland, and shelter from the north wind. There is also a track that might be for a goatherd, but only eyes such as mine could find it."

"In the foothills yonder?"

Cephan looked to the moonlit horizon beyond the darkening steppe.

"Aye," the falcon replied, "You see the peaks that lie beneath the great white star? If you were to keep them before you in your march, and if you found the way most directly between them, then you would come up into the valley where he is."

"How many days march?"

Phaedra preened herself for some minutes, and when she answered her voice was muffled by the downy feathers under one wing.

"For a fit man, alone, three days. For you, with - your dog, - it must be more."

Khan felt the hand on his collar, and kept a dignified silence.

"We are grateful." said Cephan.

"I care nothing for your thanks."

Phaedra tucked her head under her wing, couched herself down on one foot, and fell as much asleep as a falcon may.

She was still perched on the pack saddle the following dawn, when the traveller came to load his mule. He filled his water skins at the stream, packed the flour, oil, and rice that remained, balancing the burden carefully and checked the harness. Then, with his staff in one hand and the halter rope in the other, with Khan pacing behind and Phaedra rocking gently to the gait of the mule, Cephan began his march.

He left but little mark of that first camp site behind, nothing but the ashes of his fire, and grass trodden down where the mule had grazed. In the years that followed, other men pitched their tents there, because of the stream and the shade of the scrubby trees that grew there or not, as the chance of centuries of rainfall and drought dictated. They too left no lasting trace of their passing. In recent years, however, men came with machines, great coughing monsters that belched exhaust fumes to the sky, cutting slowly across the virgin earth and leaving behind a concrete highway like a merciless girdle over the steppe. They paused on that site to build a culvert above the stream, that now bubbles up unseen into a damp dark in the place where all those centuries ago Cephan laid his bed beside it, under the stars, and waited for a falcon.

After four days, they reached the foothills, and began the climb to the hidden valley. Phaedra came to report that the red horse was grazing there, tranquil among his mares.

"I wonder at your return," Khan said sourly "since you regard us so slightly."

"You, I regard not at all," she replied, "As for your master, his way by chance is mine."

That night, Cephan camped within sight of the herd, and saw that the stallion watched him until darkness fell. By morning, he was gone, and Cephan followed up the valley and camped once more, a little closer to the herd this time. The red horse watched again, but ventured some little way toward him and stood on a knoll with his nostrils flaring for a clue to this man, to his purpose, to any threat he might pose. He had been pursued many times before, but his hunters had come in bands, with baggage trains and swift horses. This man had one mule, and a hound, and he never moved but slowly.

That night, the red horse moved his mares to a safer distance. The following day he saw that his solitary follower appeared again, and at nightfall set his camp a little closer. The stallion looked suspiciously on, then came trotting up over the plain. The hound raised his head, but the man went on cooking his food.

For horses are very curious animals, as the reader will know, and it was this simple truth that Cephan had used to his advantage.

Khan watched him silently. The mule, now tethered, pulled at his rope in the shadows. Cephan stirred the rice in his cooking pot.

The stallion's wide nostrils brought him the smell of the hound, the man, and the fire. He put his head to one side so as to better view the scene before him. His ears flicked back and forth, searching for sounds that might mean danger. He heard only the night wind, the fluttering of the fire, the bubbling of the pot, and the mule moving uneasily at the end of his tether.

With one great hoof he raked the ground, declaring his presence and inviting attention, perhaps combat. The traveller put more water to heat on the fire. This the stallion watched, and then he raked the ground again. The traveller did not look up, but he spoke, quietly, as if to himself.

"You are welcome here."

The stallion was gone in an instant, and the traveller heard the urgent drumming of his hooves as he fled to rejoin his mares.

Cephan sat contentedly. The stallion had come sooner than he had dared to expect, and now, more quickly, he would come again.

Phaedra came planing lazily down the sky.

"Greetings, Phaedra." Cephan murmured, as he tended the smouldering fire.

The falcon preened in silence on her pack saddle perch.

Khan growled softly. The mule snorted. Cephan was aware of the horse, standing red-bronze beyond the firelight, but he did not raise his head. Time dripped away. The horse came closer.

Cephan did not move, nor did Khan. Phaedra preened busily, as if to show that the matter was beneath her notice. The horse put his great head down, his nostrils flaring, and moved one step toward the small tableau by the fire.

"Well met once more," the traveller said, "There is nothing here that will harm you. You need not flee."

"I fled because you amazed me, and I was afraid," replied the stallion.

Cephan stared at the glowing embers before him. He did not look directly at the horse, knowing that horses do not like to be eyed in that way by strangers.

"I mean you no harm," he said.

"Nor I," said Khan, seeing how the horse regarded him.

Silence. The horse considered. Finally he spoke again.

"What are you, to follow me as you do?"

Cephan poked absently at his fire with a stick.

"I am come to take you." he replied.

The horse stiffened, and made to turn away. Then he gave a low whinny of laughter.

They came before," he said, "Troops of riders, with baggage trains and mares to entice me, and ropes to trap me. All sent by the great king, but sent in vain! So now comes a man on foot, with a hound at heel, who leads a mule! Who sent you?"

"I am sent by the great king, but I am not his servant."

"Then who are you?"

"My name is Cephan. Men call me the Horseman. I am come to ask you to consider, whether you might wish to return to the king."

The stallion snorted in amazement. Here was this man crouched over his fire, who could speak the Word, who had an enormous wolf for a familiar, who was suggesting that he might go back to his thraldom of his own will!

"Here in this land," he said, "I am king."

The man by the fire did not look up from the flames, but he shook his head.

"But like all kings," he replied, "you must fight for your crown. Have you not seen your own get grow, colts that will grow strong as you grow weak? The horse you vanquished when you came to take his mares fell to the wolves in the winter, I would guess. The wolves and the winter will wait for you too, my proud beauty, if you abide long enough."

The stallion tossed his mane.

"Here," he said, "I am free. And freedom, to a horse, is next to life."

"I know it," Cephan replied, "Freedom is a gift from the gods, but heavenly gold tarnishes on earth. Do you not find it so?"

The small fire danced alone in the dark, and stopped the stars from falling. The strange gathering of animals was listening, - Khan and the mule and the horse. Even Phaedra had stopped her preening and now sat on one leg with her head cocked.

"Do you not find it so?" asked Cephan once more, and this time he looked directly at the great, red horse that now had come so close that he might have touched his muzzle. The horse shifted uneasily, but did not reply.

"I ask you," Cephan continued, "if it is not sour now, this freedom?"

The stallion considered.

"I must sweat, being a mortal horse, but thus is life ordained."

"Not so. Not for such as you." Cephan replied sadly.

"How so?"

"You were not born to roam the steppe, like the wind. You were born to serve, to carry men in battle, to be to them a friend, even a saviour. Men fell on their knees before your forefathers to give thanks, so fleet and beautiful were they. No-one comes to worship you - - in your freedom."

And we, being horsemen all, can see how shrewd was the blow. For have we not all seen the old horse turned out in his final pasture for one last summer? How he seems to understand that he is not wanted any longer, that there is no work for him, no rider for his stiff, old frame? At last he has his liberty, to dream away the summer under the old chestnut tree. But it does not suffice, and we see him with his head over the gate, looking out wistfully for a man to ride him!

The horse tossed his head.

"I do not seek to be admired for my beauty or rewarded for my service!"

Phaedra gave a raucous caw of approval.

Cephan looked to the fire once more, one side of his dark face polished like a hatchet by the red light, the other in shadow.

"You are young," he said softly, "and proud. Go then, back to the steppe, and never feel the hand of man upon you."

The horse grunted scornfully.

"You do not tell me of the great king's granaries, of the sweet hay in his lofts, of the mares I might enjoy."

"Nay," answered Cephan, "You would disdain such trifles."

He put water in his pot, and placed it over the fire, as if there was no more to be said. The horse did not move.

The mule was listening still. Khan was staring up at the huge presence that towered above him, too close now for him to be easy. Phaedra suddenly extended her long, pale wings and then folded them again.

"You tell me you have no place at the hearths of men," Cephan said, "even such a hearth as mine. Therefore, go with my blessing, and may the gods watch over you."

So saying, he extended his open hand, and the horse saw the small biscuit he offered. He lowered his head and took it with his soft lips, just as he had so many times taken bread from the hand of the great king.

For a horse is a remembering creature, and his habits, once learned, are never truly discarded. And so the stallion became for a moment once again the pampered darling of his royal master, and stood and chewed the biscuit with enjoyment.

Cephan hunched over his pot.

"Do not tarry here with us," he said, "for the night comes on, and your mares are left unprotected."

The stallion seemed to go, and then he turned back.

"Shall you follow me, come the dawn?"

"Nay," Cephan replied, "To what purpose? You have chosen, and so let there be an end."

The horse arched his neck, his mane a red-gold tumult, and then turned on his haunches and was gone. They heard his hooves, first trotting on the stony ground and then the drumming of his galloping feet as he sped up the valley to join his herd.

Phaedra roused her feathers and sank on one leg, for all the world like a barnyard hen roosting.

"You will never capture him now," she said happily, "He scorns your kind offer of drudgery for a ration, and empty praise for his beauty. He is no fool, your horse! He is of my kind, not of mankind! He was born for the steppe, as I was born for the sky."

Cephan did not reply, but Khan, panting gently by the fire, spoke thus:

"Not so, Phaedra. He is no simple assassin, with not a thought beyond a full crop and a safe perch. You may spurn a man's care for you, even though he comes to the great king's hall to find you, but a horse will ever cherish a kind word and a gentle hand, and will delight to carry a rider as well as he is ridden."

Phaedra sneered down at him from the pommel of the pack saddle,

"Like you? Like a humble dog as thou art? A mongrel to find meat in the shambles when you cannot kill your own?"

Khan was up in a trice, his jaws agape and his tail lashing furiously.

"I kill where and when I choose! But more than that, O bag of feathers, I have taken a master of my own choice, whom I serve because I love him, and so I am greater than thee!"

Cephan had a hand on Khan's neck, and pulled the angry hound down beside him. Phaedra had opened her wings, but she folded them again, for the darkness was now complete and her resting place made.

"Peace, my children!" Cephan said, "Enough of this folly!"

All this time, the mule had stood, silently listening, his head low, just inside the circle of warm light while his body was lost in the shadows.

"But he will come to you. It has long been foretold," he said quietly.

These were the first words he had spoken since their journey began. He knew he must carry his burden, however heavy, for as far as he was led, and that he might be fed and rested at the end of the day's march by the man who led him, if he was fortunate. Such had been his life, like the life of his fellows, and he expected nothing more. If he had ever remembered a time of freedom at his dam's side, that memory had long been mislaid along endless dusty trails and mountain passes. Besides, a mule, though a raucous animal in the baggage train, is a lowly, manmade creation, the offspring of a horse and an ass, and is not to be heard when the Word is spoken. So our mule had listened but had been silent. Until now.

Cephan stared. The mule watched them all, sadly aware how little they had considered him.

"As was foretold." he repeated.

"When?" Cephan asked.

"Do you not know the prophecy?" asked the mule.

Cephan shook his head. "Nay."

The mule looked at Khan, where he lay at his master's side.

"Nor I." said Khan

He turned his long, grey head toward Phaedra.

"I regard not the fables of men."

"I think I heard it first," the mule said reflectively, "some years ago when I was one in the baggage train of an Arab merchant and we had made camp near Aleppo. We were en route to Samarkand. I was picketed next to a lame old mule who knew that his time was near. We talked to while away the hours, and he told me of the prophecy. They came to lead him away, and I saw them whip him to see if his lameness would mend. They took him, and the pariah dogs followed, and he did not come back. He called out to me, as he was led away saying, "Remember! Remember the prophecy!"

After that, I came to hear that cry many times.

And there were those who believed this prophecy, that it would come true. I remember one night, being off-saddled at an oasis near the Oxus River, having to listen almost until daybreak to a young camel picketed nearby who told the whole camp all about it, and what would happen to us all when the time came. He was a strange animal indeed, he was, with that manic glint in the eye that you learn to dread when your own earthly hope is simply to survive."

The mule paused, considering.

"It surprises me," he said to Cephan, "that you have not heard the prophecy. For I know you are a traveller."

"My master," said Khan, "does not listen to the tittle-tattle of the baggage train."

Cephan, crouched and still, said nothing. It was Phaedra, forgetting her disdain for mules, who spoke next.

"What is this prophecy? And who was the prophet?"

The mule had by now come entirely into the firelight, and stood with his head and neck low and his long ears at rest.

"The prophet? There are many prophets. We of the mule train had one, it seems, and the camels have their own, as you would expect. Even the oxen who pull the plough hark to one of their brethren who foretold the coming as he died under the yoke. But however many the prophets, they tell the same tale."

The creatures about that lonely hearth were as still as the stars above them. Nothing moved but the small flames there, and the silence was profound. Somehow, it was understood that only Cephan could break it, and finally, he did.

"What is the prophecy?"

The mule seemed lost in a reverie of his own, and Cephan repeated the question.

"I beg your pardon," came the reply, "I was remembering the old mule in the camp near Aleppo. I will tell you what he told me then, as best I can recall it.

It is foretold that one day all the creatures of the baggage train - all the asses and the mules, all the camels and the oxen, - will be freed. The burdens will be lifted from their sore backs, and the harnesses that have chafed their sides will fall away. There will be shade in the noonday, and water in the wells, and all men will depart, never to torment them again. But they will go on foot, for all the horses that bore them shall also be spared the halter and the rod from henceforth. Horses shall never again draw their chariots or carry them into battle. And there will be a sign, not long before this comes to pass."

Here, the mule paused, and shifted uneasily, as if unsure if he should continue.

"Go on" said Cephan, and the mule looked away into the darkness.

"A horse will come. According to some he will come from the desert, and if you journey in the Arab lands you will hear it so. Others have it, that he will come from the east, and will be guided by a star. But as the tale was told to me, he will come from the steppe."

At this, Phaedra mewed like a cat in her mirth.

"A tale indeed! The dreams of those born to be slaves!"

She struck out with the talons of one foot at the wooden pommel of the pack saddle on which she perched, to show her angry scorn.

"Go on" Cephan said, one side of his face like the bloody blade of a hatchet in the firelight.

"Some say he will be a chestnut horse, and one or two say he will be sorrel, but as I heard it that night near Aleppo, he is a red horse, a red-gold horse. And he will be our god, to sustain us, as men make their gods to sustain them."

"All sorts of horses can be all sorts of colours," Cephan said, staring at the fire, "and some change colour for the winter coat. It means nothing."

"As I have said, he will come from the steppe. But he will have been born in a palace, and have been the pride of a king. So goes the prophecy, as it is told."

"How will it be," asked Khan, "that the horse, when he comes, will end your bondage?"

"That is not known," the mule replied, "Perhaps there will be a great war and men will fight until all are gone. Already they live only for blood, and killing."

The mule nodded apologetically to Cephan.

"Please forgive me."

There was silence for a while. Phaedra fell asleep on her makeshift perch, and Khan dozed with his head between his paws beside his master. Then the mule, as if disturbed by memory, suddenly spoke.

"He will bear the thumb print of the god who made him."

All horsemen know this tale, so it will be familiar to you, and you will have seen the mark on many a horse's neck, on the nearside where the neck comes up from the shoulder, a curious dent - like the mark a thumb might leave in soft clay. And you would answer, as Cephan did,

"It means nothing."

He thought, then he said,

"I did not see the mark upon him."

"You did not look for it," said the mule, "But I looked, and I saw it there."

"So," said Cephan, "does he bear a name, this messiah of yours?"

The mule, who like many of his brethren had no name and was rather sensitive on the subject, replied stiffly,

"Names are not important."

Nonetheless, this mule has become important in our tale, and so merits a mark of distinction henceforth.

The traveller shrugged, and then pulled his cloak about his shoulders. The fire was fading, and Khan, unbidden, slouched off into the darkness on patrol.

Cephan, curled in his heavy robe in the lee of an earth bank that he had scratched for himself, and with his feet to the ashes of the fire, slept ill. More than once he muttered in his dreaming, and Khan, lying at his side, lifted his head, and then let it sink between his paws. He had heard his master cry out in the night many times before.

Come the bleached dawn, Cephan seemed to assemble himself like a child solving a puzzle of old sticks and a few rags, and blew the fire to life. His hands trembled as he put his pot to boil, and he knew that the fever that had stalked him these past days would soon take him, and he cursed his ill- luck. He had found the horse. He had known how to touch the horse's mind, how to awaken his memory, and he had schemed how to bring the stallion to hand, if only he had time.

But it was a hope that existed fitfully. Last night, with a belly full of rice and the horse standing there like a golden god in the dark, it had burned brightly. But he might linger there for days, he reasoned now, with his supplies running low and fuel scarce, and all the while the horse would remain at the head of his valley with his mares, while he stayed in his camp and sweated out his fever.

There was nothing to be done but to return by the trail he had come, and hope for the king's mercy. Loading Mule, Cephan settled the panniers carefully on the animal's back. There must be no saddle sores there when he was delivered to his master's stables, or Cephan's own shoulders would bear the greater scars.

"Whither now?" asked Mule, as Cephan took the halter rope and Khan came loping to his heels.

"We go back," Cephan replied, and Mule nodded sagely. He had seen the fever traces in the man's damp face, and had noticed how he had gasped with the effort of lifting the panniers to the saddle. Phaedra looked and looked again about herself, as a falcon will, and then she rose on her satanic wings and was gone into the morning pearl sky. She had offered no farewell, and Cephan, of course, expected none. And yet he suffered, so very slightly, the smallest, the very smallest, regret at her un-looking-back departure. Taking the first steps of what looked to be a long day's march, he saw her become a mote in the eye of the sun, finally wheeling on still wings toward the mountains.

The sun came up behind the man and his mule, and the hound that loped tirelessly behind them. Their shadows, slight at first in the weak hours of morning, became thicker in front of them as the day advanced. Before them was the steppe and the barely marked trail by which they had come, and such shelter as they could find from the noonday heat.

And water, if the springs had not run dry. Always on such a journey as this, was the dread of a punctured water skin or a dry well or too many miles to the next river. All three,- the man, the mule and the hound,- knew this fear, which is always unspoken and always there. Cephan had his skins filled, and he knew his road, but still his mind reverted constantly to water, and to his failing strength.

The heat beat down upon his turbaned head and his thin body. His limbs moved like the limbs of a marionette, spare and stilted, with no more power than that of hidden strings. From time to time he stopped, to cough his dry cough in his parched mouth, and when he did this Mule nudged his elbow, and Khan thrust his muzzle into his master's hand, both of them begging silently for water. And Cephan went on, until he found a hiding place on the steppe, a few thorn bushes and a rock together that gave a scarce shade. He let Mule drink from one of his precious skins, and Khan too. As he weakened with the onset of his fever he cast about for kindling and found a few sticks to make a fire. The weight of the fuel, such as it was, barely matched the weight of the water drunk. While the sun was high, he sweated and trembled in the shade, and fell into a troubled rest, waiting for the evening hours when he must struggle to reach the spring he had left only days earlier. While he huddled in his coat, with sweat staining his shirt and running in the scar on his riven face, Mule, tethered in the shade, suddenly pricked his long ears and raised his long, grey head and looked back to the faraway mountains from which they had started that morning. He spoke a word to Khan , likewise at rest, and the hound at once got up to stare in the same direction. He raised his nose to the air, which shimmered in the heat, and then answered Mule shortly. Both animals looked at Cephan, saw that he had not marked what they had seen, and resumed their rest.

It was near nightfall when they made camp by the stream, and the fever finally took hold. Somehow Cephan unsaddled Mule and left him without a halter or hobble. When his mind sank into delirium the hound's great, warm body was there and comforted him. When the shadows came and the stars fell down on his wilderness, he felt the slow breath beside him.

Into his dreams, into the hot turmoil of his mind, into the dizzy tableau that intruded on the dark, there came another presence. Lying there in the shelter of some rocks, he was dimly aware of a lattice of movement, of tall, chestnut legs moving before his eyes, of a vast body above him, of a soft, enquiring, muzzle near his face and Khan growling a warning.

The fever broke next day, in the evening. He was weak but his head was clear. He looked about him, and saw that Khan watched from his place in the shade, and that Mule was grazing not far away on the steppe. And there was the stallion, standing there and turning his head to one side so that he could see better the exhausted vagabond on the ground before him.

Cephan scrambled painfully to his feet, and the stallion watched him, unconcerned.

"So," Cephan said, "Will you return to your master?"

He put out his hand to the horse's neck, but the horse turned away, saying nothing, and paced in his long stride down to the spring.

At nightfall Mule, by degrees, taking a pull at the grazing here and there and meandering along the way, returned to the camp. Cephan had made his meagre fire, and Khan had shared from the rice bowl. The stallion appeared to sleep on his feet, a shadow by the stream. The night was very still, and the stars cold. Afar off over the steppe a wolf howled.

"So," said Mule, "It seems I was right. There stands the chosen one."

"Chosen nothing," Cephan replied, "There stands a horse. Like any other horse."

Mule gave a little, mirthful cough.

"Did you ever know a horse to follow a man, and a stranger at that, for two days? And leave his mares to do it? And pasture in abundance too, in a valley like paradise?"

Cephan said nothing

"Why should he not follow, as I do?" Khan asked.

"You are a hound," Mule replied dismissively, "and he is a horse, and a stallion to boot."

Cephan warmed his hands at the fire. He was still weak from the fever, but he had eaten and rested now.

"I shall take him," he said, "back to the king."

CHAPTER 4

S irika, though now the city of a king, had retained the habits of the garrison that had given it birth. The four great gates were manned night and day by a chosen guard, and within the walls, in addition to the markets, the bazaar, the craftsmen's shops and the tall, narrow lanes where the townspeople had their modest homes, lay the military quarters, the armourers smithies, the bowyers workshops, and the cavalry stables. And like a garrison, the city came to life at dawn, heralded by the blast of a horn from the parapet above the north gate.

Dawn that day found King Parmenion in the temple, the very same temple built by the troops of the conqueror who had led them to this sudden, ragged, rocky hill on an otherwise featureless steppe, a day's march to the south of the road, not yet called a Silk Road, that formed the kingdom's northern border. The temple stood on the highest point, higher even than the palace, from which ran a stone staircase, called the Kings Way, up to the entrance. There, the visitor passed between monoliths surmounted by a carved stone horse, into a space no bigger than a granary, but flagged with white marble. No-one knew where this marble was quarried, for none was to be found in the kingdom, but men said it was the conqueror himself who laid the stones with his own hands. However that may be, the polished floor enhanced light from high windows where the wind whistled on stormy days. "Hippon is galloping a filly", said the priests privately when the tempest came, and they made haste to hoist heavy wooden shutters into place, and so cast the temple into darkness.

Hippon was the god worshipped there, the deity of the royal house and the subjects of the king, or most of them. For we speak of days long ago, before the devil put it into the mind of man, that he should choose deities for his fellows. And so, throughout the city, there were houses where offerings were made to other gods, but Hippon, time out of mind, was lord of the pantheon in the rites of Sirika and its kings.

He was a warrior god, and he reigned over the battle, where sometimes he was seen disguised as a golden horse where the fight was most fierce. So that the king's soldiers made small, furtive offerings to him in the dry-mouthed time before swords were drawn, and the archers bows were yet unstrung.

His priests said that, as befitted a warrior, he had no home, but there are men, and women too, who would tell you secretly that they had seen him move in the noon-day shadows of the ancient olive trees that gripped the hot, southern rocks below the city walls, and had heard the soft step of his unshod feet in the sleeping silence there.

That morning, the ceremonies duly performed, the king stepped out into the morning sunlight, and his waiting guard formed a file of five on either side as he made his way down the wide steps of the King's Way to the palace.

As we have seen, the king was careful concerning his guard. Like Cleitus, the young men who mustered that day were his personal choice. But unlike Cleitus, whose parentage was obscure, they were sons of the One Hundred, and from them the king chose his personal escort, for only men proved in battle who could claim descent from the One Hundred might guard the king.

The law harked back to the founding of the city long ago by the great conqueror who paused here on his way to meet his final destiny. There, he decreed with many fanfares of trumpets, he would found a city that would last forever, and there, as an offering to Hippon their god, would he sacrifice the greatest of his horses, the destrier that had carried him in all his famous campaigns. And here too, in gratitude for their long and selfless service, their valour and the love they bore him, which he abundantly returned, he would grant to one hundred of his men, as a mark of his special favour, estates on the fertile plain that surrounded his new city.

Legend has it, that the horse was sacrificed on the site of the temple, with due ceremony and the manly grief of his master. We, who know everything, may whisper that the horse had gone dead lame, although only his groom could have said so at the time, if he had not been murdered in a camp brawl.

The grants of land were made, and the baggage train yielded up some frightened girls and some raddled old whores to bear the first children of the conqueror's foundation. It was proclaimed that the fortunate One Hundred would be the best and the bravest of the host encamped there on the plain, plundering it like a swarm of locusts and dreaming of distant homes. This decree, this part of the city's history, is well remembered by the descendants of that lucky band.

That many men died of syphilis was long forgotten, while others perished of cold and hunger. No matter. History is written by the survivors, and against all the odds, over centuries, the colony became a city on that lonely hill, and from its impregnable fortress the heirs of the men that built it went forth and made a kingdom.

Though they forgot soon enough the painful fates of many of their ancestors, the descendants of the One Hundred treasured jealously, as we have said, the legend of the conqueror's favour, and made sure as best they might that it endured. The fertile estates remained a fantasy, but as they fought, first for survival and then for power, they had a singular advantage. For the conqueror, before he left them, had decreed how they must find every ten years, his successor. And they venerated him so much that his word remained the law. Indeed, some believed that one day he would return.

As men will, they proudly marked their own distinction by their dress, and in other ways. Unnecessarily, said their slaves and their subjects in those early days, for were they not all fair-skinned, and did not many of them have the blue eyes that stared, and made the tribal people of the steppe feel that they were being watched by a spirit? No need to wear a dead-black, long woollen tunic, and a black cloak for occasions of mark, such as attendance before the king. And as this elite chose their king from among themselves, they made sure that only their own sons, less and less fair-skinned as time passed, could form his guard, and bring them intelligence of palace plots and that backstairs gossip which so often precedes a regicide.

The ten young warriors who escorted Parmenion that morning, armed with short bronze swords and long-shafted pikes, all wore the black tunics of the Chosen. The king himself wore in addition a thick black cloak, and kept it close about him because of the morning chill in the air. Half-way down the steps he turned to look out over the steppe to the far-off mountains which had freed the rising sun. Below him lay the courtyards of his palace, and further down he could see the streets and alleys of the city, and the central square, all tied together in an untidy parcel by the march of tall battlements. A wheeling falcon was stooping down a virgin sky, and the king hoped that Cairphas the high priest did not see it. He had had enough of omens that morning already.

The guard gathered behind him while he leaned pensively on the stone parapet. For that morning was the first of the one hundred days in which preparations for the festival must be made. Back in the temple, Cairphas had descended the steep steps behind the altar, which steps only he could tread, and had consulted the mystery. He had, after a long, silent interval, returned. The king, who had been speculating on what Cairphas found to do down there – did he have a piss-hole handy? - had received the word of the mystery with the time-honoured formula of gratitude on his lips, and weary resignation in his heart. Cairphas had contrived to convey an apology with a twist of one corner of his grey-bearded mouth, and Parmenion had responded with a shrug that only the old man standing in front of him could have seen. It makes no matter, said the shrug. All know that the festival must be this year, that I am now the Old King with my days measured before me.

Parmenion made the first mark on the ancient slate kept for the purpose, as he would each morning make another, until the time came. The festival was held every ten years save in time of war, and at the end emerged the next king. History had shown the need for merciless tyranny throughout these tinderbox days of rivalry and intrigue.

The king, looking out to the distant mountains, considered his strength and his weakness.

He had been tyrant for nine years, and he had contained the border tribes in most of them. The lands were quiet, and the roads open. The merchants traded peacefully, the caravans brought all manner of fine wares to the city, and clever artisans worked in carefully controlled guilds. Above all, the trade in his kingdom's horses was flourishing in a world eternally riven by war and stitched together by mounted couriers.

But in Parmenion's strength lay the seed of his weakness, for mankind is contrary and ungrateful. Give the people peace, and they will use their leisure to plot sedition and dream their eternal dream of freedom. If the tyrant seeks peace within, he had best make war without, but Parmenion, give or take a border skirmish, had fought no campaign where young men might wash their spears and prove themselves worthy of that same black cloak that now he drew about his shoulders. He had made enemies nonetheless, and the merchants whispered that to pass along the road to the north they were taxed twice, once for the kingdom and again for the king's own coffers. He was old now too, and had no strength other than his crown. If an enemy should take it at the festival - - -.

He pondered this in silence. Behind him, his guard lounged on their pikes. Bred for battle like their fathers and grandfathers, they scorned toil and were dangerous at leisure. I know their fathers all, he mused, and I can turn my back on them only because they serve together only for one day in each moon and dare not trust each other. I am cursed with an army in a time of peace.

He turned away from the parapet and continued down the stone steps to the palace gate. The falcon, he noticed absently, was rising away to the mountains.

Was it four, or five years ago, he wondered, when one of the Chosen had raped a merchant's pretty daughter and caused rioting in the streets which it had been hard to subdue? For two nights the primacy of the Chosen, and his own rule, had hung in the balance before discipline overcame passion, but Parmenion had not forgotten the howling of the mob at his palace gates.

Now the city swarmed again with traders and merchants and their slaves and their women, as well as the people of the steppe who came to barter in the great market place. As he turned to dismiss his escort, now saluting him with their pikes grounded, Parmenion wished these proud young cubs would spend more time in the gymnasium, where they could fondle each other to their heart's content, and less in the wine shops where they were likely to fight amongst themselves or worse, molest other men's women..

One such young cub was Hephaestion, blond and blue-eyed and as handsome as a god, who was the son of Cairphas and captain of that morning's guard. Parmenion felt, as he always did, the challenge of the young man's presence. Hephaestion. If ever the gods made a prince in waiting, it was him. Unsurpassed as an athlete, a fine man on a horse, he was born a leader of men. Popular with his fellows but respected by his seniors, Parmenion knew how soldiers vied for a place on his patrols, how proudly they rode behind him.

Would he dare to challenge for the kingdom when the time came?

From the terrace of his palace the view, with the sun now climbing above the far steppe and the mountains that seemed to yearn to follow, seemed truly for a tyrant to enjoy. This, the sweep of his hand might declare, is mine. Parmenion surveyed it without pleasure. How is it, he asked himself yet again, that here, where I share the sight of eagles, I have the spirit of a sparrow?

But the slave girl who brought him bread, with his cheese and olives, and poured his wine from an earthenware flagon, saw no such misgivings. The eyes were faded a little, and he had had his head shaved to avoid the indignity of baldness, but her master carried his kingship well. He turned his iron mask of a face to look at her, admiring her beauty as he had done when she had been first brought to him. It had been a long time since he had taken her, she being always cold beneath his body. Perhaps he should have had her beaten to a more generous frame of mind, but he had seen that she wanted only to suffer, and to die. There was a boy in the palace, they said, which must be his. And so his mind moved to the matter of another son, this time a more important one.

Mylon, his first born, by a wife given to him in marriage by a king of Tartary to cement a peace after some inconclusive border dispute. The peace had not lasted, and the wife had been not quite what she was said to be, unless, drunk from the wedding feast, he had been mistaken and the bed linen had lied. He had had to rape her that night, which made it surprising that the boy - -his son? - - was her life's treasure. Two more sons had followed but both had died, one in the cradle and the other exposed after the priests had pronounced him a cripple. The rest had been daughters. Although there were five more sons by different palace girls, Mylon remained the only male issue by an acknowledged wife.

Now he must try for his father's throne and make good his claim when the time came, For this, and this alone, had Parmenion bred the golden stallion. Even without such a horse, the lad must succeed.

The lad Mylon. There indeed was the rub of it. Despite his twenty-five years, Mylon would always be just that – a lad. The court said he had inherited his mother's looks, - her raven hair, her wide cheekbones and her straight nose, - but his looks were not so important in these mixed-blood days, save that a father prefers to see his own image in his son

Mylon was a favourite in the women's quarters, where he learned to sing and to play on the lyre, and he had a sly wit that they enjoyed but Parmenion mistrusted. The father had had the son soundly thrashed for his adolescent crimes, and the son had come to hate him. He had been educated in the school and in martial exercises with other boys of rank, and had seen service, admittedly under the watchful eye of Cleitus, on the eastern border. He had killed his man in combat and could take his place in his black cape among the Chosen. But he completely lacked the instinct of command, of care for his own position. Parmenion had never forgotten the day when he had gone unexpectedly to the riding ground outside the city, to see the young men exercising their chargers. Where was Mylon? Sitting with the grooms, chatting happily away, with his horse asleep in the shade. Remembering it now, Parmenion curled his lip in silent contempt.

Looking at the sundial, he saw how rapidly the shadow had moved. Not long now before in council he must proclaim the games that would decide the fate of a kingdom, and his own.

Not long ago one could still walk, as Parmenion did that morning, from the temple down the broad stone steps, and pause as he did to take in the view of the distant mountains beyond the steppe. It was a favourite place for photographs and video footage, and the honeymooners never failed to stop there. One could continue, as he did, down to the palace gate, and pass between the broken stone remnants of the pillars there, then venture onto the terrace where he would break his fast in the summer days. It got so crowded that the authorities erected an ugly iron railing at the brink of the void below, at the bottom of which still lie the heaps of broken bottles and rusty cans.

And we can reveal that although the altar in the temple has been correctly identified, and the worship of the god Hippon discovered,(although mistakenly linked by some scholars to the cult deities of Rome), still by a quirk of fate the steps behind it, down which Cairphas descended that morning so long ago, have not yet been found. Whether this is because of the heavy flagstones that were hurriedly dragged over the entry in the last hours of Sirika, or because of the negligence of the archaeologists, we do not know. Suffice it to say that the noisy centuries have passed over that hallowed space where Cairphas consulted his mystery, and left it in silence.

CHAPTER 5

T hey had begun the morning as a trio with one following behind, but as the long march back to Sirika continued along the faintest of trails across the steppe, the trio became a quartet as the follower gradually caught up. And a strange quartet it was. A thin stick of a man leading a pack mule was not uncommon, but the loping, wolf-like figure behind the mule was remarkable, and even more so the mighty, golden horse who marched with his long-limbed stride beside the hound.

Cephan appeared not to notice the addition to his party, trudging on with Mule's lead-rope in one hand, scanning the distance in front of him, his mind busy with nomad concerns. He had filled his waterskins before leaving that last camp with the sweet water from the stream, but he knew that it was a long march to the wells ahead, and that even the deepest wells might one day fail. Also, Mule was beginning to go lame. Only slightly, but enough to slow the march. He had bruised the sole of his near fore foot, he said, and could limp on for some time yet, but finally he would need to rest. When they came to a scant shade of rocks and scrub, with the sun high above them, Cephan made camp and off-saddled him.

He attended as best as he could to Mule's forefoot, made a shift of a dressing that he drenched with precious water, and then let fall the hoof from between his knees.

"Thanks indeed," Mule grunted.

"We must go on, at nightfall, to the wells" Cephan replied.

"I know it," he said stoically, after the manner of his kind.

He rested his sore foot with a sigh.

"And so to Sirika, with the horse. According to the prophecy."

"I doubt," said Cephan wearily, "if yonder horse knows anything about your prophecy."

If mules could shrug, then Mule would have done so.

"You could ask him yourself, as he travels our way."

Seeing Cephan coming, the horse pricked his ears and his nostrils flared for the man-smell, but he did not move from his place in the shade.

"It pleases me," said Cephan very quietly, "that you abide my company."

"We take the same road" the horse replied.

"I shall take you to the city. To your master the king." Cephan said "And to return the mule, which is his."

"That mule no more belongs to the king than I belong to you," the horse answered "but he suffers his bondage in silence, being betrayed, like all of us, by the dog."

He turned his chestnut head to Khan, who lay not far off, listening to this exchange, and who now took up the challenge.

"Not a dog," Khan snapped "for in me runs the blood of wolves! "

"Peace, my children!"

Cephan waved his scarecrow arms, causing the horse to shy violently. Khan rumbled in his throat.

For the lore of the baggage train, as all pack animals learn at their mother's sides, is that it was a dog that was the fount of all the grief and suffering of beasts of burden since the world began. For then all animals were free and there was but one man and one woman, who lived by a waterhole in a desert and were near to death. In the evening, when the ox and the ass, the donkey and the horse and the camel, came to drink, the man begged them to save him and his woman. But the beasts saw how the man's eyes glittered white, and his tongue flickered in his mouth like a snake's, and they sensed the evil in him, and went away. But that night there came a dog, and the man gave him a bone that he could not crack with his own weak jaws, and in gratitude the dog showed the way from the desert, and the man and the woman survived. Thus, their descendants came to rule the earth, and on the trails and the mountain passes, at the watermills and before the plough, in mines and quarries and cities, the beasts of burden have paid the price for the dog's folly ever since. For, decreed the lore, if the man and the woman had perished then the stain of their evil would never have spread over the earth.

Not because of the cruelty meted out to an ass, or the neglect of a camel, because the lore also decreed that the weak would be the prey of the strong, and that mankind is strong in schemes and trickery there can be no doubt.

But because for many generations the creatures of the baggage train have watched, and been the silent judges of mankind. Horses have carried men, or drawn them in their chariots, to meet in killing places and to spill their hot, red blood upon the ground. Mules in their hundreds have laboured over mountain trails laden with the supplies of armies, and seen the men who led them sweating in fear. Camels of the caravan, couched at the wells at night, have gazed aloof at sudden treachery and the chance medley of sworn friends.

And the beasts of burden have seen that man desires to claim for himself even the very earth and the sky. He wishes not only to ride his horse, to drive his mule, or to rule his oxen. He will fight all comers to prevent another from doing the same, and he will make a mark with a hot iron on the animal's tormented hide to say, "This beast is sacred to me, and I am a god." But he is no god, for gods do not come to the stillness, as a man does, and gods are not afraid.

For the creatures of the baggage train know that stillness, the strange departure by countless ways, that leaves a body behind, sometimes maimed or starved or worn out by toil, and sometimes young and perfect. They do not fear it, for it has not come to them, but they see that men are afraid of the stillness, and will beg, or pray, or scream to halt the falling blade, or turn and run, trying to outstrip the swift arrows and the seeking spears of the advancing host.

And yet they will kill, and kill again, to banish their own kind from some piece of earth, even the desert sands or the impenetrable forests, and in their vanity and their folly they make walls and gates to mark their kingdoms. They will conjure their own gods, and make sacrifice, and struggle against the stillness, and will pass away without honour. And the beasts of burden will watch, just as I have said. Those camels couched for the night at the well, those mules silent under the stars in their pickets, cavalry horses awaiting the trumpet at dawn, oxen out-spanned beside the plough, elephants rattling their leg-chains in the lines. All awaiting the quick coming of men with creeping hands and clever fingers, and those white- glitter eyes in the morning. All at a loss to understand how the dog could have betrayed them so, and all uttering that same quiet curse that the chestnut horse had made.

Which is why Cephan had a warning hand on Khan's neck, and why Khan trailed his stern unmoving between his hocks, knowing the bitter jest of the baggage train, that dogs wag their tails because they are still grateful for that bone.

"Shall you go with me to Sirika?" Cephan asked the chestnut horse.

"I see no other trail than this." the horse replied "to Sirika."

"You could go back" Cephan, his eyes dwelling on the horizon far behind. "If I were a horse, and as free as you are, I would not go to Sirika, or the haunts of men."

The horse also looked back to the mountains, and perhaps he remembered his mares, and the cool streams, and the pasture. Then he turned his head away.

"Only yonder lies a trail." he replied, "and a horse, like a man, will follow a trail."

"You need no trail," Cephan whispered, "You may cross the steppe as a bird crosses the sky."

"Yes," the horse replied "but you may lead me on this trail. It is ordained."

He stood there in the hot noon, as still as a figurine, his red-gold hide dappled by the shade, and Cephan gazed at him while the silence ran out like sand between fingers.

Behind him, Mule coughed on a dry straw. Cephan turned away and went to spread the saddle blanket in the scarce shade, and lie down. Khan settled beside him.

"Well?" Mule said out of the side of his mouth, still snatching at the withered grasses nearby.

"He comes with us" Cephan replied shortly.

Mule's jaws ceased for a moment, with his bony, long -eared head drooping between his legs, and then he continued his foraging.

Rested, they went on, with Mule moving stiffly and the chestnut horse sometimes before them and sometimes behind, until later that day, when his pace seemed to slacken. Then he stopped, and raised his head. His nostrils dilated, first enquiringly and then in alarm. He snorted.

Cephan, looking to the thin trail in front of them, saw that it ran into a small valley, and that a herd of goats lay there in the shade, peacefully chewing their cud, with a thin wisp of a lad watching as they approached.

Khan looked hopefully at the nearest goat. Mule rested his foreleg. Cephan turned to see the stallion transfixed, his legs trembling and his tail aloft like a flag on a staff.

"Gently!" Cephan cried, "Only a few goats that cannot harm you!"

The horse gave a nervous snort, and then trotted back the way they had come before he halted, irresolute. Cephan sighed, but another stop for Mule would not come amiss. He retraced his steps some way, off-saddled him, and squatted down on his blanket. In the distance he could see the goatherd watching.

Eventually, the stallion stood before him, still alert and uneasy.

"Why such trouble, over a few goats?"

"I know not," the horse replied, still looking along the trail, "Maybe another time - - I cannot tell. But the stink of them seethes in my head. Their eyes, their strange voices take me outside myself, and I am lost - - -."

Ah," Cephan murmured "I have known such terror, in my own time."

"Is it so?" the horse asked disinterestedly, "I doubt that. You being - - what you are."

But he had shifted his attention now to the man who squatted before him, who said, as if he thought aloud,

"I have seen the weak become strong in their fear."

The stallion snorted once more.

"I am not weak! But yes, when such terror takes me I cannot be ruled, nor rule myself. And then I am mighty indeed!"

Squinting up at the horse, seeing the huge chest and the powerful arch of the crest, the mass of the animal carried on those lethal hooves, Cephan rose carefully to his feet.

"We go on now," he said, "And you will be brave. But not closer to those goats than you can abide them. We shall come with you. And Khan will not be tempted either! Eh, Khan?"

"And look," Cephan continued, having learned long ago, when dealing with horses, to turn a difficult situation to his advantage "how I can help you choose your way."

He took from the pack saddle a long rope, and knotted one end into a halter.

"This part comes up over your nose, so - - - -. do not fret, for it cannot hurt you. So. Good. And now this, over your ears. Gently! There! You are a brave horse indeed!"

He patted the stallion's neck.

"Now, see. You may follow me, and I shall show you where to go, so that the goats will not trouble you. That is why we use these halters, to make the way easier. As Mule here knows full well, eh, Mule?"

Mule looked at him askance.

"And that is why you must suffer these things, to guide you only, so much as you consent to follow."

Another reassuring pat.

"For clearly no man's power can prevail against yours."

Cephan stepped a little way, holding the rope end.

"Come."

He gave the slightest, the most gentle pressure, and then, after a moment,

"Good! Very good! So, now we can go on, and I can show you the way."

Camped that evening, with the light just beginning to fail, there came a sudden fall of wings and talons striking, and Phaedra composed herself on the saddle bow and looked about her. Cephan offered her his arm, and she hopped to his wrist with a low croak of pleasure, then back again.

"Well met!" said Cephan

"Indeed," she replied, "for I bring news that will pin back your ears."

Having said as much, she began to pluck absently at her snowy plumage.

Cephan poked at his fire silently. Khan, who had raised his head to watch her descent, let it fall again with a weary sigh. The mule and the horse, alarmed for a moment, grazed on. Phaedra continued to draw her breast feathers through her terrible mouth, and for a long time there was silence.

"Well?" Cephan asked finally.

The falcon gave no sign of having heard the question.

"I beseech you," Cephan said, "to be charitable to your humble servant."

Phaedra tucked a feather back into place, folded her wings carefully, and eyed him coldly.

"Well," she said, "but the dog must not hear."

She hopped once more to Cephan's fist, and scratched the back of her head delicately with the back talon of one foot. The four hooks of the other foot tightened on his wrist, and she ruffled her plumage again.

"The king has proclaimed the festival, where they choose the next king" she said.

"When shall it be?" Cephan asked.

"I know not," she replied, "for I abide the seasons, the heat and the cold, the dark and the light. I do not crawl upon the earth and fear the passing time."

"One hundred days" Khan said quietly.

The falcon hopped back to the saddle bow with an angry cry and turned her back on them.

"I know of the games," the hound went on, "for once when I was young, I was taken there to fight. In a pit, For my life."

Cephan stared at him.

"You never told me as much."

71

"There is much that I have not told you." Khan replied, "I did not get these scars in -- - - -."

His ears flattened against his skull, and he stopped.

"In the place where I found you" Cephan finished for him.

"No."

Phaedra, ghost-pale on the saddle bow, twisted her head to blink at them.

"And I forgot to say, there is a cavalry patrol bivouacked yonder, some distance along this road. Towards the city."

CHAPTER 6

T he old king had a visitor that night to his private chamber, where there was a brazier full of red charcoal against the evening chill, scented with a sweet, sappy wood brought from the mountains. Its warm light was taken up by rush lamps and the floor was strewn with heavy fleeces, brightly dyed. A huge, cedar chest stood in one corner, and the king's own arms and armour were stacked in another. There was a long settle made of ebony and inlaid with gold, where the king reclined. His only companion was an old wolf-hound bitch, stretched out before the brazier. On one wall was a long curtain, and it was from behind this curtain that the visitor stepped, after a preliminary cough, very quietly. The wolf-hound raised her head for a moment, and then let it sink again between her paws. She had seen this visitor many times before, who came by night, bearing arms even in the presence of the king. He advanced now, raising one arm in salute, and stood in front of the king's couch.

"Well, Cleitus" said Parmenion, by way of greeting, and a little dwarf crept out of the shadows bearing a flagon and a bronze goblet. Standing in front of Cleitus, he drank from the flagon and stood there for a full minute. Then he poured wine into the goblet and offered it to Cleitus with a low obeisance.

"Thanks, Tosto" Cleitus said, taking it. The dwarf retreated silently to his corner. He could not have replied even had he wished to do so, for he had been dumb from birth.

"Drink, Cleitus my friend," said Parmenion, "It is a good wine. It may serve to sweeten bad news, by the look of you."

"Not bad news, sir," Cleitus replied, fetching a wan smile, "It is the steep steps that make my old legs tremble."

"Then drink," said Parmenion, "and then you can tell me what they say in the city."

Cleitus drank, then wiped his lips on the back of his wrist with a sigh.

"Good wine indeed," he said, "We don't drink this down at the gate. " Not" - he added hastily, "that it's over-watered, what they give us."

Parmenion thought he would find that out for himself before the world got much older.

"What news?" he asked abruptly.

"It is well received, Sir, that your son should make his claim. They say in the taverns that it must be this year or not at all, given the time that has gone, and your son being no stripling now."

The king's thin lips twitched in a rueful smile. He always had the plain truth from Cleitus.

"And do they say," he asked, "how he goes about the business"

"Not time yet to say much about that, Sir. But he has been to the quarters, and they have all promised him their voices, and the merchants say they will match what he gives in the way of wine."

"Did he go in person?"

"Indeed, Sir. On the day after the games were heralded. To all men of note, so none could say they were slighted."

Parmenion nodded slowly, his mind only a little eased. A promise is like a flower, went the old adage. It must be plucked firmly, and in good time.

"And did they greet him kindly?" he asked, prodded by his own misgiving.

Cleitus, standing on the other side of the glowing brazier, looked down on his reclining lord with a sad kind of anger welling in his breast. He was no courtier, and the question, he felt, was not a fair one. Seeking time for thought, he drained the goblet and had scarce looked about him before the dwarf was silently at his elbow to take it.

They did, Sir," he answered, "as anyone would expect, he being your son."

Parmenion looked away from him, and stared at the red charcoal that gave life to his thin, pale, grey-whiskered cheeks. What did he want me to tell him, Cleitus thought bitterly. About the greeting of Sorbon, one of the chief men of the merchant's quarter? That over-friendliness, bordering on disrespect. That hail-fellow arm about the shoulders, that should have earned him a thrashing? And would have done, had he tried a trick like that on you in the old days, he said to himself, looking at Parmenion who now seemed to huddle in front of the brazier like an old man.

"They must be kept up to the mark," the king said slowly, as if he addressed the coals, "An empty promise is easy made and easy broken."

"Your son must shift for himself, Sir," Cleitus replied.

Which was the unhappy truth of it. And without the colt. He went on.

"They say, it will be a fair contest now, your son not riding the chestnut horse."

It was the wisdom of the taverns and the barracks, that the man who rode that horse would be the king. Some said there would then be no true contest at all, and that the old king courted the anger of the god by making a spectacle of a sacred contest.

"There are men out at the theatre already," Cleitus continued.

Parmenion nodded. He had ridden out that day, to the same site chosen by the founding conqueror centuries earlier. It lay below the city down a paved avenue between tall stone pillars. From one side of the arena the ground began to rise into the hill on which the city stood, and here the terraces had been laid out where the descendants of the Chosen gathered. A crescent of stone rose to the high podium where the king and his retinue would watch the games. On the opposite side the plain ran away to the steppe, and here the common people of the city, the traders and the travellers, the stall –holders and the jugglers, vied for position behind a timber barrier. There they settled with their friends and family to watch, to drink, and, as the festival came to its noisy climax, to jeer at their betters over on the other side of the raked sand of the arena.

"They say Sorbon has put forward his son, Sir." said Cleitus.

He spoke abruptly, thinking the news would be unwelcome, anxious to spit it out. But Parmenion merely nodded again.

"The man had the grace to tell me to my face," he said, "And such a son might at least become a throne, though he will never be a king."

Sorbon was a member of the council. He was rich, highly regarded in the merchant's quarter where he had been born, and he was ambitious. Not for me, he would say with his fat chuckle, for how could such an old barrel of lard like me sit with dignity on the throne of the great king? But my son is such a man. I sometimes wonder if his mother did not betray me with a god!

As well she might have done, men thought privately, while they smiled at his old joke. She was a daughter of a family that could claim unquestioned descent from one of the Hundred, and her mother had wept bitterly to see the girl given to Sorbon, who came from nowhere with his moneybags and his vulgar ways.

But the son might well have been, as his father said, begotten by a god, although the mother and all her kin claimed that he was the image of his maternal grandsire. He was named Antheus.

He had green eyes, in a land where most were brown except for those touched by the legacy of the Hundred, whose eyes were often blue.

Having served his time in a cavalry patrol on the eastern frontier, he had seen combat and had killed his man, as they said in the barracks, and so he wore the black cape of the

Chosen.

But he was no soldier, and he had no intention of squandering his life in some ugly border war. Spoiled and petted since birth, he had come to believe that he was a king in waiting, but he craved power only for its own sake, and would never be of service to a kingdom as a king should be.

Power is best wielded by a man of courage, but Antheus was not brave. As a child he had endured the taunts of other boys when he fled from playground brawls. And when a horse was led from the stables by the old Tartar slave who was to teach him to ride, he had felt his guts churn with a fear that never entirely left him when he sat in a saddle. But he had learned to hide this from other men, if not from his horses, and in some ways he was indeed his father's son. He was not only unprincipled, he was also ruthless, and by his birth on his mother's side, he was entitled to try for the kingdom.

As Parmenion well knew, couching there beside the brazier, on which Tosto had just shovelled more red charcoal.

"Others?" Parmenion said, "Besides Antheus?"

"Two more, Sir" Cleitus replied, shifting uncomfortably. A slight gesture by the king sent Tosto to his side with the bronze goblet. The captain drained it gratefully. This was uncomfortable work. He wished himself back in the tavern.

"Well?"

"They say, Sir, that young Hephaestion is pushed to it by his friends. And that Bessus is named contender with Hin-Sho at his back."

Parmenion shook his head.

"The son of the high priest! How can that be? If he wins, it will be said he had the blessing of the god. And if he fails, the victor will be thought accursed, to have stood in his way!"

"If you talk to his father, Sir - - -"

"Cairphas will have spelled it out, no doubt. How would it seem, if I forced my own son's rivals to withdraw?"

Not for the first time, Cleitus thought that not for ten virgins would he change places with his king. He gave his cup back to Tosto, and remained silent.

"And Bessus!"

"Yes, Sir."

"That drunken old scamp! Dishonouring his family for the price of a drink!"

Parmenion's voice had risen in anger, and the wolf-hound bitch raised her old head enquiringly.

"There, there, Julia. Good girl. If only men were as faithful as you!"

Parmenion brooded over the brazier, and Cleitus stood erect on the other side of it. In the shadows Tosto kept his own dumb counsel and watched over the lamps.

"Bessus! He has nothing left but his name to sell." said the king.

Certainly Bessus had made much of his famous ancestor. History had it, that centuries ago at the city's foundation, the leader of the One Hundred had been one Bessus, so named in honour of one of the conqueror's great generals. For countless generations the blood of Bessus had often coursed in the veins of the kings. Parmenion himself had taken power from the grandfather of this present Bessus.

Who, one fine morning, when he was young, had been leading his patrol of horse along an empty, mountain stretch of the north highway. Behind him rode ten men, and beside him another, who bore the tall banner by which the patrol could be instantly identified. These banners had been carried time out of mind by the patrols of the kings of Sirika, and never had one been lost in an engagement where any member of the patrol survived.

Bessus' error was to dismount his men too close to a dry watercourse in the heat of the midday. His ill –luck was that it sheltered, purely by chance, a band of tribesmen from the mountains. In the brief but bloody struggle that followed, every last man of the patrol died except Bessus, who was taken prisoner.

Men said Hippon might have been more merciful, and ordained his death at the head of his command. But he was ransomed by his family, and came home to live as the only man to have lost a banner and survived.

Needless to say, he never rode out again, as he had done on that fateful morning when life was so full of promise. His father died soon afterwards, heartbroken, and Bessus was head of one of the first families of the kingdom. He squandered his fortune on women and boys, and opened his house to all the riff-raff of Sirika, all the gamblers and the whore masters, all the sharp horse-traders and the men from the eastern caravans with their strange drugs. By the time of which we speak, he was little more than a brothel-keeper and an opium addict, and he owed his soul to a Tartar horse-dealer named Hin-Sho.

But, as Parmenion had said, he had his name, and the right to ride his horse and perhaps win a kingdom.

"Bessus! How will he ever sit on a horse again?" he said.

"They say he is under lock and key, though he cries out for opium. And he was a good man with a horse before he lost his banner. And Hin-Sho can buy the best, Sir."

The king looked at his captain with something like hostility, and Cleitus stared sullenly back. You asked for the truth, he thought, and nobody else will tell you. You poor old bastard.

It was the king who looked away first, ostensibly to search for Tosto, who was waiting in the shadows.

"More wine, Cleitus. And I will come down to the gate tomorrow, to drink your ration with you there."

When Cleitus was gone, and the hanging carefully drawn across the wall, Parmenion lay staring at the red charcoal of the brazier. The more contenders the better, of course, since men could be persuaded, bought, or threatened, in different directions. Three rivals for the throne was better than one claimant, since they could divide the disaffected among themselves, and each become less powerful in the process. And with so many, how could it be said that he had tried to pre-empt Hippon's wisdom?

Of the three, he feared Hephaestion the most. He was good-looking and a promising soldier, even if his father was a priest. And though he could not spend freely, or pour drink down the thousands of ready throats that would pack the streets of Sirika, he had that assurance, that gift for command that ensures obedience. Parmenion thought that Cairphas must be brought to see sense.

He did not fear Bessus as a rival for his son. Men would allow themselves to be stroked but they did not like to be taken for fools. And Bessus was no more substantial than a shadow- puppet on a wall. All men knew that the light behind it was an unknown Mongol from the steppe with a good eye for a horse and a retinue of cut-throats. They would drink his wine, but would not be ruled by such a one.

Then, there was Antheus. Green-eyed Antheus. Of a good lineage on his mother's side, and with his father's money behind him. And the backing of the powerful merchants quarter, where men seemed to have forgotten that they traded their horses in peace and profit only so long as the Chosen kept the land of Sirika in something like tranquillity. Sorbon, already a member of the council, was well placed to drop a word here, or silver there, or a cautionary whisper aside to a man who seemed unsteady in support of his son. He would never let his own ambition show, and by the time men saw that they had a profligate boy for a king it would be too late.

For Sirika needed a soldier- king, just as that long-gone conqueror had foreseen. How else to rule such a land, with ever-restless tribes in the north, the threat of invasion from the east, and those camel-riding nomads from the deserts in the west? Not to mention the southern borders, from which patrols, and sometimes greater forces, unaccountably failed to return.

Then Parmenion thought what the fate of his kingdom might be in the hands of his own son, and his face twisted in silent anguish. How could he have fathered this sly, cunning young waster who bewitched the women with his songs and was fit only to be a minstrel?

Because for all his faults, Parmenion ruled only to preserve what he had taken and to pass on his land to one of his own kind, not to this misbegotten lad who, he had always suspected, had been sired in Tartary before his mother became his queen. As he lay there in the darkening chamber, as the lamps burned out one by one and Tosto, overcome by sleep, snored in his corner, Parmenion brooded and considered, speculated and dreamed, until finally the old wolf-hound bitch whined and padded off to the door, where one of the guard took her away to the kennels. And so he went to his bed, sending away the girl who waited there, and slept.

CHAPTER 7

In the dawn-dark the horse slept on the edge of wakefulness, head low and one hind leg at rest, some little way from the ashes of the fire where Cephan stood and looked out along the trail, now just discernible, snaking thinly away through the steppe. Khan watched, accepting the briefest caress upon his heavy, scarred head. Phaedra slept like an old hen, squatting upon the saddle bow. Mule was grazing.

Cephan pulled his long coat around his shoulders.

"So," Cephan said to the horse, "to Sirika, when the day comes."

The horse puthered his breath calmly through his nostrils.

"And the patrol?"

"I must meet it on the way," Cephan replied "Mule is lame, and my provender gone. Also, there is no water, until the city. But for you, there is another way."

He gestured slightly toward the horizon where the dawn came, slight and silently. The horse looked, and saw the infant day.

"The way back - ," he said.

"You must go now," Cephan said "or come with me, to be given over to the king. You will be treated well, but never freed again. If you resist them, they will abuse you, and your life will be one of suffering. If you obey, you will be a slave, and your soul will shrink in you like an empty water skin."

The words came unbidden to his tongue. He heard them in amazement, heedlessly chattering away the only advantage that remained to him in the world. Then he saw how the first light of day had made so splendid the mighty animal before him, and he knew why he had spoken thus. Such moments take a man unaware, but leave him a little closer to his gods.

"You must be gone," he said, "for if I am thought to have taken you, and then freed you - -."

"No," the horse replied, "You shall lead me into Sirika."

"Perhaps Mule was right," Cephan said, "About the prophecy."

"Maybe. He is a wise one. He knows more than I what will become of me. Named only now, he has given me a name."

"Men give names to hawks and hounds and horses," Cephan replied as if by way of an excuse. "It is a thing we do. Harmless enough."

"Name me how you will," the horse said, "but to Mule, and to all his kindred, I am Messiah."

Cephan saw nothing on the trail before them, even in the full morning light, but Phaedra, who had been sitting one-footed on the saddle bow, suddenly lifted into the sky on scimitar wings.

"Look yonder."

Then she was spiralling into the wind, and rising to become a small toy hanging over the vast green cradle below her.

After a few moments more, Cephan saw the black banner fluttering, and then, below it, the band of horsemen whose coming it proclaimed. They were riding fast, and he knew that soon they would be upon them.

"Remember," he said softly to the horse, "I will not forsake you."

The horse lifted his head. Mule, limping behind them, made a strange, coughing sound in his windpipe that might have been laughter, or perhaps a curse. Khan came up by his master's side, as close as a shadow.

As the patrol moved closer, the leader lifted his arm and the troop came to a sudden halt behind him. In the silence the banner fell like a rag about its standard. Cephan stood tall to suffer the inspection of narrow, hostile eyes.

"I remember you," said the captain, who alone wore the black tunic of the Chosen. His gaze shifted to the great, gaunt animal that stood there, obedient to the halter, and then again to the skeletal, black hound that was staring up at him with its tongue lolling over its fangs. Then to the mule behind them, bearing the king's brand on one thin, bony quarter.

"It seems that you have found the king's treasure."

Cephan did not reply, part of a silent tableau, lit by the sun behind so that one shadow, black as a bloodstain, ran into the dusty road. His gaze ran over the troop before him. The captain was a veteran, by the look of him. Cephan's eyes went to the men who slouched in their saddles behind their captain. Young men, all Tartars, sloe eyed and broad faced with high cheekbones and black hair bound in braids under their leather caps, all sitting on tough little steppe horses as though born on horseback. Mercenaries, thought Cephan, who had been one himself. His eyes met those of their captain and he nodded. I know how it is, the nod seemed to say. I know how the great king your master hires these savages because the ranks of his own kind shrink with every generation. And how, with them riding behind you, your spine must flinch from the imagined blow.

"What is your business with me?" Cephan said at last.

The captain frowned. That casual nod had not been a pleasantry, and neither was this disdainful enquiry. Behind him, one or two men grinned.

"I have orders to bring you before the king," he replied brusquely, "and to take back his colt with me."

He turned in his saddle, and spoke to one of his men. The man leaped down from his horse, as nimble as a cat, threw his reins to another, and advanced upon the still motionless group before him. He held out his hand, looking warily down at Khan, at the stallion that towered over him, and at the man who held the halter rope. Then Cephan surrendered the rope, and the man turned to lead the horse away.

But the stallion did not move. The man tugged at the halter, but the horse had lifted his head, and lifted it remained. The man tugged again, but it was as if he tugged at the head of a statue. His comrades grinned, and one of them called out in their strange tongue, something that made the rest hoot with mirth. The captain gave an order, and silence fell like a blade, cutting off their voices.

Cephan watched. He knew how impossible could be the simple exercise of persuading a horse, any horse, to go forward. Even a few paces, let alone the journey to Sirika. Even an ordinary, stubborn horse. He saw that the captain understood this also, alone before his patrol, thwarted in front of his mercenaries. Cephan stepped up to the shoulder of his horse. Khan watched with his wolf eyes, and Mule looked on, resting that lame forefoot.

"If you are wise," Cephan said softly, "you will let me lead him into Sirika. And you will escort us before the great king. All of us, for this is a stallion like no other, stronger than any you can ever know, and he will come only with me, and this mule whom he knows, and even my hound."

The captain's sweating, bearded face twisted with indecision. He had given orders and he wanted to see them carried out.

"You will lose a little before your men," Cephan continued softly, "but your duty will be done. And if you should return without the horse - - , - you will never ride under a banner again."

He turned toward the man who still held the halter rope, his hand outstretched.

Perhaps, in that moment it might be said that Sirika's fate was decided. It is recorded only in these pages. That place on the dusty track over the morning steppe, has no stone to mark it. No flags of triumph save that sinister, black squadron banner and no music save the soft chink of a bit and the restless stamp of horse's feet. For witnesses, only that Tartar band, and a hound, and an old, lame mule.

For the captain gave an order, Cephan took the lead rope, and the small convoy began the journey into Sirika.

First rode one half of the squadron, then the strange party they escorted, and behind came the rearguard, with the captain to see all before him.

We never knew the name of that captain who reversed his order, seeing that to insist would be to invite chaos. But we can tell, in due course, how he died, and we know that his bones are long consumed into the windswept earth where the ruins of Sirika still stand. But all in due time. For now, we note how the course of history can be changed by the small decisions of unknown men, as happened there, as we shall come to see.

And so the stallion came slowly to Sirika, at the pace of a lame mule, led by a sceptre of a man with saturnine, unmoving features who was followed by a tall, scar-muzzled hound whose dust-dark hide seemed to have been stretched over his wasted frame. Under the great archway at nightfall they came, with the Tartars riding at the throng in the narrow way and Cleitus's men drawing the heavy gates together behind them.

Children might believe that the prophecy of which the mule had spoken was fulfilled, for the Messiah, born in a palace, had come indeed from the steppe. As had been foretold.

In the courtyard of his palace Parmenion waited, with his court about him. And because he was a king, he could not betray the leap of tenderness within his breast, the exultation that for a moment almost overwhelmed him. How strange, that this pitiless, loveless man, this cruel tyrant who could look upon the slaughter of defeated men and the torture of his enemies without pity or remorse, should be now enthralled by this vagrant colt's return.

"Looks as fit as the day he was taken!" said a courtier, choosing not to mention the stallion's thin flanks and staring ribs. "His coat as bright as gold still!" another said, smiling, discreetly silent about the scars upon it, legacies of the stallion's battles for his mares.

Parmenion said nothing. Too late, he thought now as his joy abated. A summer, a winter and a spring had passed since the horse was stolen, the festival was already called, and here was the colt upon which so much depended, as yet unbroken. And there had been rumours, faint but insistent, of an army building far to the east beyond the lands of the Tartars. He had sent two squadrons on reconnaissance, and neither had returned. He had spies travelling east with the merchants, but had received no word from them.

Surely, Parmenion had cares that the return of a horse, even such a horse as his golden stallion, could lift but little from his mind. And where was Mylon, for whose sake he had bred this mighty creature, who could carry the son to take the father's crown? Was he in the courtyard to see the colt return? Not he. Drinking with his friends, Parmenion supposed glumly as he sat in his hall.

But still, he sent for his old, Arab horsemaster and learned that indeed the stallion was strong and healthy, none the worse for his adventures even if scarred about the head and neck and sadly in need of the farrier. The desiccated old man said he had a secret remedy that would smooth away the scars in no time. The horse's mane and tail would be trimmed, and with good forage and a well-littered stable, he would be fit in a few days' time to be brought before the great king.

Parmenion murmured a word that might have been thanks, then made a dismissive gesture. The man standing before him hesitated.

"The mule, my lord. The mule that was given for the use of this Cephan, who brought back the horse."

"What of it? He can take the mule for his own. Did I not say so?"

"Indeed, my lord. But the mule is lame, and needs care. The man wishes that my lord might take back the mule."

Parmenion smiled, despite his troubles.

"And he will take his pick, we suppose, of the stables?"

"No, my lord. He wanted only a goat."

"A goat!"

The courtiers smiled nervously. It was difficult to know, in these uncertain days, what response might chime well with the king.

"Yes, my lord. For his hound, my lord. To feed the brute."

"And did you give him a goat?"

Parmenion was no longer smiling. Looking up at his grim visage, the old groom could only pray that his answer would be the right one.

"Yes, my lord. For you ordered, my lord, that the man should have all he desired."

"Well then? A goat for a mule, even a lame one. See the animal is well treated."

The old Arab bowed, and then looked defiantly up to the king's chamberlain, who stood behind the throne.

"Then I have obeyed my lord's wish, and I can have no greater happiness than that."

The chamberlain, an obese eunuch gowned in a green, woollen robe and wearing a silver chain of office, glared back.

"Let him tell my lord what became of this goat" he hissed.

The horsemaster spread his hands wide.

"I gave this Cephan a goat, my lord, as you desired."

Parmenion saw that men about him smiled. The chamberlain was not popular.

"Well then," he said wearily, sensing he was about to be assailed with trivia from both sides, "what did become of the goat?"

The chamberlain's voice wobbled with indignation.

"My lord wished this Cephan, who brought back the stallion, well treated. I did all that was possible. But he would not come to the kitchens until he had seen the horse stabled. When he came, with the cooks half asleep with waiting, he wanted to feed his devil dog that never leaves him. The cooks had already given the bones to the pariahs in the yard. So he went back to the stables and took the goat, and led it to the mendicant's quarters where I had clean straw laid for him, and robes also, and I had turned out the two holy men who rested there. Then he cut the throat of the goat right there in the doorway, to feed his devil dog. Now he lies on his bed, eating like a wolf what he took from the kitchens and drinking from a wineskin, while his hound devours the goat in the open doorway, and the beast will not suffer me to approach his master!"

The courtiers tittered. The old Arab wailed.

"I did give him the goat, my lord, just as you wished. I could not - - ."

"Peace, Abdullah!" Parmenion said impatiently, "You did as you should have done. There is no fault in you."

"I asked," said the chamberlain, "did he want a woman, and he said he was tired. Then I sent a slave girl with water for him to wash himself, for he smells like a fox, and he fondled her breasts and made her cry."

"You did well, Nooran," said Parmenion, "you have behaved just as I would wish, being my envoy to this man."

The wily old eunuch caught at the chance opening offered by the king's own word.

"Indeed, my lord, as you say, I am your envoy - -"

His eyes, creased up in his puffy face, glinted malevolently down at Abdullah, and he paused to emphasise his standing, before he continued,

"And he thinks of me as such, perhaps because of my bearing. Accordingly, he asked if he would have an audience with my lord. After he was rested."

"Did he now?"

The courtiers murmured in astonishment.

"And what answer did you give him, Nooran?" Parmenion asked.

"I told him," the chamberlain replied with great dignity, "that he would be called when he was wanted."

The response was met by approving nods, but Parmenion saw the man hesitate, and he knew there was something else.

"Go on," he said softly.

Nooran swallowed hard, and his cheeks flushed.

"He told me - -that is, he threatened me, my lord, -- that if I did not do his bidding he would injure me in some way."

"Go on."

"He said, my lord, that you will need him bye and bye, and that he cannot wait long upon your pleasure."

Parmenion raised his goblet, took wine, and dabbed at his bearded lip with the napkin offered by a boy.

"Put a guard in the passage outside his door. Two men, at all hours."

He stood up. Men stood away to either side.

"And Abdullah - -."

"My lord?"

"See to the breaking of this stallion. There has been time enough wasted already. I want him for my son, you understand. I bred him, and my son will ride him at the festival. You have ninety days, you understand?"

"With such a horse - - - ."

"Ninety days."

"Yes, lord."

CHAPTER 8

Khan, full-bellied and rank with the smell of goat, called from the doorway by his master's whisper in the dark, settled with a satisfied grunt beside the prone body under the blankets on the straw, and felt the hand that pulled tenderly at the remnants of one ear.

"You told how it was, that when you were young, you fought in a pit, at the time of the festival?"

Khan feigned sleep.

"When Phaedra came down, and we had made camp, on the way back. She said the king had proclaimed the festival, and you said you had fought in a pit, for your life."

It was but a half-drunk murmur, but there was a caress too, and the hound whined, and shifted his huge bulk in the straw.

"In the days before I found you."

The voice was very quiet, but insistent, and the pull on the ear a little stronger. Khan saw that his strategy would not avail him.

"My youth was long ago, master."

There came a chuckle in the darkness.

"Not so long ago as mine, Khan. And not forgotten. Tell me how it was that you came by these scars that my fingers can trace even now upon your skull. And your neck, just there --."

Khan sighed, and for a long time was remote in the deep of memory. Cephan, knowing that a hurt mind must not be pressed, waited. At length, he heard the hound's voice in the night beside him, strangely small in so great a body.

"I was whelped in the land of snows, far away to the north of this place, where sometimes at night the day mocks the moon with veils of light wonderful to behold. Phaedra hunts there on her passage, and I too was bred to hunt. The wolf - - -."

Silence. Cephan is warm and still, but his mind twines with the mind beside him.

"My mother said, there is wolf in me - - -. But I grew - -became - -what I am. I was taken then, and sold to a merchant to guard his gate. I lived at the end of a chain, and his children stoned me for their amusement. But one day, the chain parted, and I killed his little daughter. I still recall the sweetness of her blood on my teeth."

"Let your spirit be still, Khan," came the soft answer, "for the pity and the shame of it fall only on mankind."

"They came at me in the courtyard. The merchant wanted me taken alive so he might flog me to death. He screamed at his men, and was screaming still when I tore out his throat."

"You did well."

"In their panic they had left the gates open, and I fled. For a while I ran with the curs in the alleys and the markets, but there is no hiding in a pack for such as me. I was trapped with nets by the watchmen, and they sold me to a trader who brought me here, down the mountain passes and across the steppe."

Silence once more, in that stone cell, in that dark corner, in that stink of goat and sour wine, in that profound communion.

"If you render me your memories," Cephan said gently, "then I will take something of your pain."

"In a cage. And he put me to fight in a pit. By then, I had killed many of my own kind. Once I killed a bear. But it fell out that no man would put his dog against me, so I was not worth the meat to feed me. It happened that at the time of the festival, there came a prince from the plains beyond the mountains. He bought me, and had me taken to his palace, this time carried by an elephant across those white peaks. I remember the cold, even I, who was born in the land of snow!"

"And it was there," Cephan said softly into the shadows, "that I found you."

"In another cage," Khan went on, his words coming more easily now with his tale well begun, "was I kept. In the menagerie of the prince, in the cellars under the palace. At first he would come to look at me with his friends and his guests. His ladies came too, attended by their eunuchs, to twitter to one another in their amazement at my size, and my appearance, and the scars that I bore. I was fed from a silver dish with fresh offal from the kitchens. Until I was a novelty no more, which was not long. Then only the keeper came, and after him his slave, when he was told. There was a tiger across the passage, who wanted me, being half-starved, and he would go up and down, up and down, behind his bars, coughing all the time in his hunger. And I own, I was afraid. That the bars would keep me in I discovered well enough. But it was long before I understood that they would keep him out.

There was no time in those cellars. No day or night, only shadows and torches and footsteps and the distant sound of the horses in the stables. The tiger patrolled his bars less and less, and finally lay down for ever, and was still. After they took his body away I was alone. I wished for nothing, waited for nothing, suffered thirst and hunger, - - - .

And you will know, master, that for all living creatures it is thirst that is most terrible - - - . I would lick at the floor where it was damp with my own piss, to ease my tongue in my jaws - - - . And then you came."

Khan lay silent, his muzzle seeking his master's hand in the darkness.

"I came," Cephan said, remembering, "to discover the passage, where it led, in case of need. Such a passage, in such a cellar, saved me when I was a boy. And I knew, though I was overseer of the royal stable, that I was hated by the household. So, I came looking. And I found you, so weak that you could scarcely raise your head."

"I expected nothing," Khan replied.

But you looked up at me when I raised the lamp, Cephan thought. And maybe that it why my heart went out to you, that you expected nothing.

"You went away, and then came back with water. Fresh water. And you drew the bolts and brought it to me, where I lay. And waited while I drank.

And then you came again, and again. Each time you came into the cage, which amazed me, for I could see that you carried no weapon. When I grew stronger, you brought meat. In time I came to wait for the water and the flesh. And then, strangely, I came to wait for you. It pleased me that you should come. At last you laid your hand on my head, and the soft weight of it eased my spirit. It has done so always, and it does so now."

Cephan smiled in the dark, remembering how many times his courage had nearly failed him, hearing the warning rumble from the throat and the lift of the lip above the long fangs.

"We came together, thou and I" he said.

"I came to know it," Khan went on, "as I grew stronger, and you bid me follow you in those stone passages, farther and farther as time went by, even to the stables where the grooms beheld me with curses when they thought you could not hear."

"Rats in a barrel," said Cephan, "never in front of a man, but always there behind. I knew I should kill one."

"And I knew, when you came for me that last time, that now I must follow wherever your shadow fell upon the earth."

If he were a man, Cephan thought, stretched beside his hound's quiet body, it would be a lie. For Khan though, it was the simple statement of a simple truth.

"Your road with me has been a hard one," he whispered into the dark. "You have hungered. This last journey with the horse, I thought your belly would shrink to your backbone."

"It mattered not, as I followed you. What becomes of the horse, master, now he is gone from us?"

Cephan chuckled.

"Wait, and we shall see. But I promise you, my friend, we shall have better lodgings than this ere long."

"And another goat?"

"As many goats as you can eat. Or at least as many as are good for you. I would not wish for a fat hound."

For two days and nights Cephan waited. He was brought good food and wine, and he slept away the hours with Khan slumbering beside him. In the passage the guards changed. Finally Abdullah, the king's horse master, came to look cautiously over the prone but watchful hound in the doorway.

"I expected you before now," Cephan said. It was morning, and he sat on his mattress cross-legged, chewing on his bread.

"The king commands me," Abdullah, replied, "to seek your help."

Cephan smiled his one-cornered smile. He saw that the old man was unhappy, and he could guess the reason.

"Surely," he answered, "the king must know it is your duty, not mine, to train his horses."

"Indeed," Abdullah replied, "I have been honoured with my lord's trust for many years."

And he drew himself up.

"Well then," Cephan said, "you must go about the king's business."

Abdullah swallowed.

"The king has commanded me - - -."

""As you said," Cephan interrupted, "Now, why should that be?"

"The horse," the old man said, "the stallion you brought in from the steppe, is - - -. Is - - - -."

He spread his hands despairingly. That he, Abdullah, acknowledged in all Sirika as a man so well versed in the ways of horses, so consummate a trainer of the most wayward of them, must come at the king's command to seek the help of this strange vagrant, was a blow to his pride from which he hardly expected to recover.

Cephan nodded.

"Is more than you and all your men can manage. Has he killed a man yet?"

"He savaged a stable boy only. But the king is impatient - - ."

Again that awful smile, the scar lifting one side of the face as if it was a hairy curtain.

"Kings are impatient. It is how the world turns, my friend."

"My lord wishes the horse trained as befits one so mighty and so beautiful. Indeed," Abdullah went on, forgetting his own misery for a moment, "it is a horse I never thought I should live to see."

Cephan softened slightly.

"I am here, awaiting the king's pleasure."

"Then he bids me say, that he has been forgetful of your needs. His chamberlain will attend you."

He turned to go.

"One more thing, old man."

"Old enough to have courtesy from the likes of you!"

"I piss on your shoes. What became of that mule, that I had from the king when I sought out his horse?"

"I know not," Abdullah replied frostily, "I do not concern myself with mules. I am the king's horse master."

Cephan gave a cough of laughter.

"You had best concern yourself with that one, old man. For if he is not there when I call for him, and I tell the king I gave you warning, it may be your back will lack a hide."

With the door open, and the heavy curtain that concealed the interior in one hand, Cleitus paused.

"What name shall I give?"

"I gave you my name when first we met," Cephan replied, "at the gate."

Cleitus pulled aside the curtain.

" Cephan, my lord. Whom men call the Horseman."

He stood to one side, and Cephan stepped into the king's private chamber. Bathed and barbered by a slave girl, he wore a red woollen tunic and soft kidskin boots. His black hair was cropped and his beard well - trimmed. The lines of his face had been softened by good food and rest, and he bore himself with dignity. Khan, for once, was sulking in his master's chamber.

The king, lying on his couch with the dwarf Tosto behind him, looked at the man who now bowed before him. It was mid-morning, and the daylight in the chamber showed the long scar on the side of his visitor's face.

Handsome, once upon a time, the king thought. Palace-bred by the look of him. How came he by that scar, I wonder?

"Greetings, Cephan."

Cephan bowed .

"The girl Phoebe allowed you enough rest?"

Cleitus grinned. Cephan nodded gravely.

"We are grateful," the king continued, "for the return of our horse. My servant Abdullah tells me that he has never before had to deal with such a savage."

"I am ever at your service - - -." Cephan began, but then was taken by a savage paroxysm of coughing that shook his thin body, and when it was over he wiped a dribble of blood from the corner of his mouth. Parmenion noted the courtly turn of phrase, seemed not to notice the blood.

"We need you once more" he said.

Cephan seemed to consider for a moment. Then he said quietly,

"There is not enough time."

"You have not heard, yet, what I require of you" said Parmenion

"We are not alone, Sir," Cephan replied.

"Cleitus is my friend," Parmenion answered, "and my dwarf is as dumb as this hound beside me."

"Well, then. You wish me to train the stallion so that your son can ride him at the festival and win your throne. But, Sir, there is not enough time for that."

Parmenion raised himself on one elbow.

"Yet you thought of it yourself," he countered, "and you are no dreamer of dreams."

"All men dream, my lord," Cephan replied, "and no harm in that. But what you ask is impossible."

"No," said Parmenion, "Not to you. Not if you wish to help me."

Parmenion made a small gesture, and Tosto, understanding him perfectly, brought forward one of the great, ebony couches. Another, more expansive wave of his hand, and Cephan came forward to take it.

Palace born, Parmenion thought again, seeing how gracefully the man laid himself down.

"I am already beholden to you for the return of the colt" he said "And if you can help me now - - -."

Parmenion made another expansive gesture with his open hand, indicating his generosity.

"You must tell me, how it lies in my power to repay you."

When Cephan did not answer, he went on,

"Think on it. You are my honoured guest. My house is yours. And think of the glory of it! My poor Abdullah will hang himself, and such a triumph will be yours!"

Cephan smiled, not that sardonic hitch of half a face, but a gentle curl of his lips.

"A taking idea," he said, "but see how high are the stakes!"

Parmenion shook his head.

"Many kings have ventured all in battle. And in battle, all may turn on the conduct of a horse."

As we all understand. We spare a moment in this narrative to pay silent homage to the forgotten horses of war. They who drew the chariots, who carried armoured knights to the field, who bore the lancers and the hussars of yesterday, who charged the infantry squares - and went down before their deadly hail. The teams who drew the guns, and the fleet chargers of the gallopers. How many died, horribly mutilated and in pain on earth stained with their own blood, we shall never know.

But to Parmenion, considering his quandary, and Cephan, already despite his words thinking how it might be managed. The two men, the king and the vagrant, had eased unconsciously together now, their heads close, their words soft. Cleitus and the dwarf were forgotten. Only the old bitch, Julia, heard the exchange that followed.

"If that horse carries my son from the festival, he will come home a victor. There will be no-one to deny him his triumph, and I, his father, will be as safe as a snail. That is why I bred him, so carefully and at such cost! His dam from the Fergana valley, and his sire from the deserts. If I had not been robbed, then there would have been no man in the kingdom to venture against my son!"

"Then you must tell me truly, how he rides, this son of yours."

"He sits a horse well enough."

We all know how it is, to be damned with faint praise.

Cephan understood the king's words clearly. For some time there was complete, unmoving silence. Then he nodded.

"I shall need that old mule."

"As you wish"

"And at the end? If I succeed?"

"Whatever you desire."

"And if I fail?"

The old king shook his head.

"Then you must make your peace with my enemies."

Mule was picketed in a long stall in one of the king's yards, with animals to either side of him. Well fed and well littered, he had been able to lie down, which had eased his legs and allowed the injured fore-foot to heal. His emaciated body had begun to fill out, and now he stood quietly chewing straw, apparently oblivious to the stable sounds about him, but in reality waiting to discover by every footfall, every stir along the picket line, every human voice in the yard, a warning of what might befall him next. The mules to either side had left him in peace since, days ago now, he had come limping in, but the rumour that came with his arrival, whispered up and down the line in the nights that followed, had made their forbearance no easier. Now one of them, on the near-side, plucked up his courage.

"They say," he ventured, "that the horse is come."

"Horse?" said Mule, "which horse?"

"To fulfil the prophecy. The horse that came in with you, from the steppe. The king's horse."

Mule went on chewing.

"Is it so?" said the off-side beast.

But Mule did not reply.

"They say," went on Off-side, "it is foretold."

Still Mule was silent.

"You may tell us. We will say nothing" said Near-side, and Mule turned his wise old head to look sadly at so blatant a liar.

At that moment the picket line began to stir, with men carrying harnesses and an overseer shouting, coming down the line to choose his mules, prodding backsides with his stick as he went.

"That one, and that one. I need twenty sound mules, and I get a choice of cripples!"

Mule rested a forefoot ostentatiously, but it was too late. He was led out of the line along with his neighbours, and within minutes was haltered and saddled. Cautiously he twitched his hide against the girth and the crupper, arched his back to discover how the saddle sat along his spine. For him the fit of his harness was more important than the weight of his load.

"Here we go again," he said. "Another tribute party, I should guess."

"Easy going out, but coming back will be no joke" said Off-side, lashing out casually at the lad who was pulling up his girth.

For there was scarcely a mule in Sirika not worked in the collection of the king's tribute from the tribes. Necessary taxation, the rulers of Sirika decreed, for a land well-governed, free for the great horse herds, at peace within its own borders and protected from enemies without. Robbery, said the tribes. Extortion at the point of the sword, the bleeding of the weak by the strong. It had long been so, muttered the elders of the villages as they collected the grain, the olives, the grapes and the fruit that went to feed the warrior race who ruled Sirika from their mountain city. Oh, for times long past before the locusts came!

Nothing of all this mattered to Mule. For now, the empty panniers were not a burden, and he was led to his place in the line. His harness fitted well enough, and he had been watered at the stable cistern. At the head of the column, the overseer mounted his own mule, and gestured with his stick. The gates of the compound swung open.

A shout, a hurry of feet across the stone flags.

"We could be lucky," Near-side said hopefully, from his place in front of the mule.

"You don't begin until you've started" Off-side replied from behind.

Down the column came the overseer, with a palace servant by his side, both looking intently at the mules, examining the brands on their rumps.

"All the same!" the palace flunkey said despairingly.

"Well fancy that!" the overseer replied sarcastically, "When you think they are the property of the same king!"

And indeed, the mules all bore the brand of the monarchs of Sirika since time immemorial. It was a high-shouldered lozenge topped with double inverted crescents, and it was called the ox-head mark.

But a groom identified Mule as the animal that had been brought in, lame and spent, days ago, and the flunkey, trying to sound knowledgeable, said that indeed it was a fine, upstanding mule, which made the overseer spit his contempt for the opinion of a houseboy. Mule was led out of the line and unsaddled.

"Lucky you!" Nearside muttered.

"Spare us a thought" said Off-side.

But the Mule was too wise to think himself lucky, and certainly he had no sympathy to spare for his erstwhile companions. Back in the picket line, there was the barley straw.

CHAPTER 9

In the palace garden was a raised stone pool, a perfect marble circle where Cephan sat and trailed his fingers in the water, and watched the shoal of silver fish motionless under the lilies. It was a tranquil place, made between the ramparts and the colonnade that sheltered the king's apartments, where few came save the slaves who tended the fruit trees in their great earthenware urns, which gave shade from the sun, now high in the burning heavens. Beyond the walls and far away, when the keen eye had traversed the soft, grey-green folds of the steppe, it fell upon the mountain snows of the horizon, like a white lace trimming to the edge of the world.

The girl Phoebe came silently, her shadow short and dark on the stone flags. Somewhere in the pillared shade lay Khan, half asleep in the noonday heat. Phoebe was beautiful, taken in a raid on a caravan where the merchant had thought to pass through Sirika without paying his dues. She was the daughter of a defeated king in the cold lands beyond the mountains, a blonde-haired, pale-skinned, grey-eyed girl with a face like a goddess and a body that might have been created for the pleasure of men. Many were the men who had sought to satisfy themselves with her - and strangely failed. Perhaps it was that grave, silent submission that left a man feeling that he had rifled a treasure chest and had found nothing.

Cephan had watched her when she sponged his aching, filthy body with perfumed water as he lay naked, pummelling his hard, scarred muscles with expert hands, using fragrant oils. She had brought him new-baked bread at daybreak, tall flagons of water so cold that dew formed on their earthenware bellies, and bowls of nectarines, peaches and pomegranates such as he had never before tasted. She wore a muslin tunic that wrapped her body from head to toe, and she never smiled.

She was his for the taking, of course, the gift of a king to his vagrant visitor. Cephan had thought he would have her, perhaps not at once, like a greedy dog, but after he had rested a while.

And so, on the third night, he had taken her hand and pulled her, gently enough, to his bed.

But Khan, in the doorway, had girned softly in his throat, and Cephan had turned away from the girl to chide him. Then, turning back, he had caught her looking down at him, her perfect face touched by sorrowful pity.

Cephan had felt lust drain from him, extinguished like a torch in water. He had let drop her hand, and turned away. And silently she had left him.

That night, curiously, there had been born a fellowship, a lamp lit, a tiny glimmer in an empty dark, the understanding of two solitary beings that the other suffered too.

And so, this noon, when Phoebe came to him, Cephan turned his better cheek toward her as he smiled, and her grey eyes softened.

"I can bring you wine, or perhaps some fruits - - ."

Her voice was small, but hard, and she was not fluent in the bastard mix of tongues that was the lingua franca of those times.

Cephan had been watching a tame, pearl-white dove that had come to drink at the pool. She found it difficult to perch on the polished marble sill, and then to lower her pink bill into the water beneath, but thirst compelled her, and she spread her wings to balance herself.

She had no warning of her end, must have missed the reflection of the falling falcon in the pool surface. Talons like iron nails drove into her soft flesh and a hooked beak pulled at her plumage. She fluttered weakly under the falcon's pinions, gaped in agony when that hook dived into the cavity of her breast, and then died when it reached her pounding little heart.

Phoebe gave a muted scream and ran back into the palace.

Phaedra raised her grim, bloodied head for a moment, and then buried it again in the twitching body between her talons. Cephan looked cautiously about. It was noon, and not a lizard stirred in the heat. Khan, ever-watchful, had seen the kill, had seen that nothing was required of him, and had not moved from his place in the shade.

Cephan waited for the falcon to finish her business.

"Greetings!" he said at last.

Phaedra looked at him, stared at his fresh-trimmed beard and his neat, clean clothes.

"Well!" she said, "Quite the little princeling now!"

She hopped onto his naked arm, her talons red stained. Her crop was bloated, and she moved her head from side to side to settle it.

"I saw that you came back with the king's horse. Make best use of his favour now, for he will soon have greater troubles!"

"Indeed?"

But she was cleaning her feet of any scraps that remained, using the upper mandible of her beak delicately, exploring the tiny spaces between her toes. Cephan watched her, then again looked about him. Still not a soul stirred, save that he could see Phoebe staring from the shadows. Gently, he eased his forearm up and down, and Phaedra rocked to the motion of it.

"Come," he coaxed, "tell me."

"Across the eastern border, a column of fighting men march toward the city."

"Whose men"

Phaedra looked at him, balefully contemptuous.

"Soft living has made you a fool indeed. The men of the emperor who rules there in the east. He who can send horsemen across the plains in thousands, and make the old king a memory while he lies in his bed."

"Not this old king, Phaedra my beauty," Cephan replied softly, "for he is a king of Sirika. And the kings of Sirika fight for their thrones, even to their last day. He will have his forces ready, my sweet bird."

His voice pleased her, and she roused her plumage and then put one foot up into her breast, and seemed to rest on his arm.

"He has no forces on that border," she replied, "and that is the word of Phaedra, who sees the world beneath her wings."

She had marked Phoebe's tip-toe approach, saw her staring.

"In the land where I was fledged, there were such girls," she muttered into her breast-down, so that Cephan had to put his head close to hers, "girls as pale as the snow, whiter than my wings."

Phoebe saw how they conspired, the man with the falcon on his wrist, his thin face so close to her red-stained beak.

"This," Cephan said, "is my falcon, called Phaedra."

Phaedra ruffled her feathers crossly.

"You must be a wizard," said Phoebe, wide-eyed. "I never saw such a thing."

Cephan hitched the side of his face.

"A wizard," he said, "to put a spell on you."

He had meant to jest with her, to soften the grave lines of her face.

"Oh no!" Phaedra muttered, opening her wings, the full, fearsome spread of her pinions.

Phoebe shrank back with a gasp, then turned and fled.

"Your way with women leaves much to be desired."

With that, the falcon mounted effortlessly into the air, turned into the slight wind that came over the parapet, and was soon a black mark on the silver-blue mirror sky. On the surface of the pool in the garden floated a few soft feathers, and on the marble sill were small splashes of blood, where the tame dove had died.

And so to the king's stables in the vaults of the citadel. In one corner two stalls had been opened to make a cage, and there they had loosed the chestnut horse like a captive lion. There was a guard on the heavy, timber barrier that served as a door, and a scared groom waiting. "Lie down." Cephan said to Khan.

He looked over the barrier, and the stallion screamed a welcome.

"Open it."

"Sir! He will - - ."

"Open it."

The lad was sweating with fear, but he dragged the barrier aside, and the horse came charging forward and then stopped dead.

"Go. Both of you."

They did, the groom and the guard, fleeing thankfully down the passage.

"Well then," said Cephan quietly, "why such noise? You see how you have frightened those men?"

The stallion trembled, and his golden skin was running white foam.

"You said that you would not forsake me!" he cried.

"And here I am, to make good my promise."

Cephan moved, softly but deliberately, into the cage. The sanded floor was foul, and the space was dark and stank of horse piss.

"See how they have treated you?" he said. "Because they fear you. But it looks," he went on, staring at the mighty creature keenly, "that you are fed well enough. Khan here, would say you were fat! Eh, Khan?"

Khan let his tongue loll over his teeth, panting his agreement, and the horse seemed to be comforted by the sight of his trail fellow.

"Fat, but very dirty! I suppose you have denied them entry to your prison, O my savage?"

Messiah rolled a sullen eye.

"Come," Cephan said lightly, running his hand down the horse's neck, "enough of this nonsense. And from such as you, the Messiah! Such an example! Have you no shame?"

"You come late."

But the horse was calm now, and Cephan went on caressing him, speaking softly.

"I had to wait. Until they found out for themselves what you are, and that they needed me. And it seems you have taught them well enough, for even Abdullah - - .."

"Abdullah! That old fraud, with his foul ointment that he wanted smear on my scars! He might use it on his backside if he likes, on the marks I left there."

Cephan tutted, stroking the horse, checking his legs for signs of injury, running his fingers down either side of the spine, watching for the tell-tale flinch. Nothing. He sighed in relief.

"They have not hurt you. Which is good, for there is much to be done."

"There is indeed! Clearly, I cannot stay here, in this cage."

"You were born in a stable. Much like this place."

"But now I have been free and have wandered the steppe and have seen the sky above me and the stars at night, and I am become kindred to the winds."

Cephan looked at the great horse sadly, knowing that he spoke the truth for himself and all his kind. He knew how a horse craves liberty, those times when his head goes up and his nostrils widen and he looks into the distance and seems to see more than the distant hills.

"But you came back," he replied gently, "to the place where you were born, and the men who made you. You came with me freely."

The golden head turned toward him in the gloom of the stable. Outside they heard quick footsteps, and Abdullah's thin, reedy voice.

Cephan spoke quietly to Khan, who paced away down the passage. Abdullah shrieked a warning, and the footsteps receded.

Messiah stamped one huge forefoot in the dirt impatiently.

"You are a fool," he cried, "Will you take me from this hovel where you left me?"

"We leave tonight, for a little farm not far from the city, belonging to the king, where we can be private."

"And why must we be private?"

Cephan, who had trained horses all his life, felt the fear in his stomach.

"So that I can show you how to carry me" he replied with a badly feigned nonchalance.

"Carry you? On my back?"

Cephan put out his hand to pat the arch of the horse's neck reassuringly, then let it fall.

It was he who needed support.

"Indeed so."

Khan , down the passage, rumbled in his throat. Abdullah was waiting at the end, peering fearfully, with a bevy of supporters.

"With a saddle? Messiah enquired, "and a bronze bar in my mouth?"

Cephan was silent, looking at the height of the horse's wither.

"You brought me here in the night," Messiah went on, "and now you take me out again, also at night. To a private place, as you say. Why so?"

His eye rolled enquiringly, white in the gloom.

"The king," Cephan replied, "desires secrecy."

"Secrecy! There is Abdullah there, down the passage, who will gabble like a goose. And the slaves whisper to strangers, when the guards look away. Whatever else I am, or may become, I shall never be a secret."

"We go tonight, or not at all," Cephan said firmly, "and I must see you cleaned, and shod. I will put this halter on - - so, and you will stand quietly while the boys do their work."

And Messiah did stand quiet, and Cephan called Abdullah and his slaves, and the horse was washed clean of the filth of his stable, his mane and tail were pulled tidy, and his great feet were shod.

"Now," Cephan said, "I leave you. Until nightfall, when I will return. With a friend of yours."

Mule was there, on the picket line in the shade, pulling on the straw heaped before him. A line of animals to either side stood to the long rope, eating or resting, with their tails switching constantly because of the flies. Cephan stepped quietly to his head, and Mule snorted softly in recognition.

"Well," he said, through one side of his mouth, "all good times end. Where to next?"

"We leave tonight," Cephan whispered, "But not a long trail."

"Not to the east?"

"No. Why do you ask me that?"

"Look down the line," Mule replied, "to my right. The grey mule. They brought him in two nights ago, about dawn, scarcely able to walk and his saddle wet with man's blood. We could all smell it."

Cephan glanced sideways.

"I see him," he muttered, "Not branded."

"No," the Mule replied, "but he carried the king's spy, and what a tale he tells! For his master, seeming to be ready to carry a load for a ration, fell in with the followers of a force that has crossed the border. It is commanded by an envoy from the great emperor of the lands in the east, and the spy was in his camp when there came by night another whom he knew."

Mule chewed busily. Cephan waited patiently until he resumed.

"Another of the king's spies! Greeted by the envoy in person, and taken to his private quarters! Our man thought to slip away at dawn, but he was seen by this turncoat and followed to the lines where our friend there waited. The two men quarrelled."

Another interval, this time a lengthy one.

"Go on" Cephan said at last.

"Don't rush me. Our man accused the other of treason. Turncoat said he was fighting for freedom from tyranny, that the old king must be overthrown, and that his true master was Sorbon, whose young son would bring fresh blood to the throne, and rule not by fear but by consent, just as Alexander had decreed - - . "

Mule considered this. Cephan waited.

"Anyway, our man was stabbed as he turned to mount, and then again in the thigh as he fled. Knowing the lie of the hills best, he escaped his pursuers, and his mule carried him home. Whether his rider lives, the mule does not know, but they took him into the palace."

Cephan stood in silent wonderment, shook his head, reflected. The same old tale, he thought. The same words. Freedom against tyranny. Youth against old age. No fight for me.

"So," Mule asked, "If not east, where then?"

"We go south" Cephan answered, "but a few leagues."

"With the chestnut horse. He whom we call the Messiah?"

"How did you know?"

"I am old now, as mules go on. I watch and I listen, and I carry my loads and watch and wait again. And I wonder. Tell me, are there many days, until the festival of Alexander?"

"Eighty four. Not as many as I need."

"Ah," Mule whispered, half to himself, "we shall see how the dice roll now."

CHAPTER 10

If we could peer through the fog of legend and tradition, forget the songs of the bards and the tales of old men, we would find that first festival a disappointing spectacle. The ground was hastily prepared under the shadow of the great rock that was to become Sirika, and volunteers were arbitrarily selected from the ranks of the army in the time-honoured military fashion, to act as stewards. The surrounding steppe settlements were pillaged for the thin wine and the fermented mare's milk of that country, along with their goats and their sheep.

There were jugglers and acrobats, the whores did well, and the quacks and fortune-tellers did good business while the games brought triumph or defeat to young men.

Finally, there came into the makeshift arena the great general, the demi-god himself, mounted on his famed charger, to display his grace, his skill, and his uncanny harmony with his horse. To touch the souls of these war-weary, half-starved, battle-hardened veterans who had followed him from homes that were now a distant memory, to remind them why they had done so, to give them hope that his promises of gold and glory would be fulfilled.

And he did just that. Proud and straight, he sat the mighty destrier that stepped high beneath him before the serried ranks of his army with his bridle-hand on a rein that might have been a silken thread and his sword hand on his hip. He carried no weapon, and he had no guard, and his troops howled their adulation to the evening skies.

Could history have been made, as it was that day, without that horse? Maybe, but not so well. It is no chance that until this final century, which is ours, great men have been immortalised in bronze or stone for ages past, all sitting on horses. Some more comfortably than others, it is true, but all borrowing the power and the glory of their steeds to make a dishonest point to posterity.

Alexander's parade set the seal on his festival, and then he rode back to his half-built temple, privately giving thanks to the gods and his groom for having kept the horse sound for one last day with the aid of some foul potion that had been forced down the animal's gullet that morning.

The temple's marble floor was his gift, stone hauled out of a palace in Persia and drawn there by oxen over mountain and plain. The oxen had been dying in their yokes of a mysterious sickness, so the stone could not be carried farther, and in any case the conqueror had wearied of his spoils.

Which is how it came to be laid in the temple, so far from any marble quarry. Excavations of the ancient city have recently revealed the stones, but their provenance is yet unknown and historians may never discover that they were first laid in the hall of a Persian king. What lies beneath them remains a secret still.

However that may be, we know that Alexander gave land that was not his to men who could barely defend it and then marched away to his own destiny. Behind him he left a temple and plans for a city to be named in memory of that famous horse. The city was built, against all the odds, but somehow took the name of the mountain where it stood, not the name of the horse.

He left, too, that strange system of government by which his new city was to be ruled. For on the very dawn of his departure the One Hundred came to him in his tent, crowding under the awning and jostling the guards, to ask, who should take his place when he had gone?

The demi-god wanted to turn his back on these forsaken men and make a start in the cool of the morning, but he was Alexander, and his every move, his every word, would be watched and remembered by the men of his guard, his servants, his chamberlain, even his slaves. They were all looking at him now.

So he smiled a regal smile, and gave his decision. He spoke clearly and without hesitation, as if the question of the governance of Sirika had been a matter of deep deliberation, instead of the hastily assembled thoughts of the moment. Every ten years, he decreed, let the best horseman among you be your chosen king That his hare-brained scheme was flawed from the outset did not trouble Alexander at all. He had no intention of being there to see it fail.

But curiously, the scheme did not fail. While the original One Hundred still lived, it was the word of their commander, and by the time they were all dead, it was sanctified by tradition. It was simple to understand and easy to manipulate when necessary. It offered to any man who could join the ranks of the One Hundred, a chance to be king. Victory in the festival went to the man who could best assume the mantle of the now long-dead hero in displaying himself and his horse in the arena and in that ride back to the temple. By their plaudits or their scorn the mob had their say, and when the priests, having consulted Hippon, announced the winner, he had by happy coincidence frequently been the choice of that noisy multitude.

And so it had come about that the kingdom of Sirika fell not to the righteous, the just, the wise, or even the brave or the victor in battle, but to the best rider ----- on a splendid horse.

There might be worse ways of finding a king. A true horseman is one who can face the truth about himself, for horses never lie, and they never flatter. He is a brave man, for these creatures are always the stronger, sometimes impulsive and given to strange whims and fancies that must be humoured and devilment which must be overcome. A horseman is cunning and declines a contest until he finds favourable ground. He is wise in that he knows the limits of his ability and his experience, and he can endure pain and bitter disappointment and yet be patient and hope for a better day. He is a man of iron self-control, and above all, he is just. For a horse has a profound sense of what is right and will remember, and not forgive, a blow struck in anger.

Perhaps such a man reads these pages, and wishes fate might have given him the chance to roll such a dice for such a kingdom!

And so we return to Parmenion's stables in that time of night that was once called the time of the dead, when there comes a creeping cold in the air and a quietness even among the creatures of the dark. Life wavers like a dying flame, and dawn is late in coming.

Along the dark passage, hardly to be seen in the shadows, came a water-boy. At that hour? Strangely, yes. He stepped over the guard, recumbent on the flags outside the Messiah's stable, who recognised him and grunted sleepily. He slowly drew the timber barrier ajar, sufficiently for him to be able to reach the water pail inside. The horse snorted warily from within, and the boy looked up and down the passage, one hand extended.

And found himself trapped between Khan at one end and Cephan, like a sceptre of doom, padding down upon him from the other. The glass phial was torn from his hand, his throat was taken in a vice-like grip, and moments later he was a prisoner in a cell where a single rush light burned and the sceptre stood in the doorway with that dreadful hound at his feet.

"Who sent you?"

He was little more than a child, a thin waif shivering in his dirty rags, and he tried to gather his wits.

"No one, sir! I came to see that the horse had water for the night. Abdullah would have me flogged if the bucket was empty in the morning!"

The sceptre in the doorway shook its head.

"Who sent you?"

The great hound crept a little closer and looked at the boy with his yellow wolf eyes.

The lad began to whimper, huddled there in the corner, shrinking from the advance of that ghastly hound.

"My mother."

Cephan nodded.

"And she gave you this?"

He held out the thin glass bottle, removed the stopper, sniffed, then looked down at his prisoner, who bowed his head.

"And told you to pour the poison into the horse's bucket?"

"I swear I didn't know - -!"

Cephan's voice was like the sudden hiss of a cobra disturbed.

"If you lie to me again, I will let go my hound and he will kill you, for you are very small, and in times past he was stoned by children like you. And he does not forget. Eh,Khan?"

Khan whined softly in his throat.

Cephan stooped, holding the feeble lamp closer, and the boy stared up at him and saw no mercy in that face, with its frightful scar.

"Who gave the poison to your mother?"

"I don't know! I swear I don't know! She goes with men at night to keep us fed. She did not tell me!"

"And where do I find your mother?"

The boy began to cry piteously. Cephan waited for a moment and then, quietly, said,

"Khan."

The scream of terror rang through the stables, and then the sobs redoubled. Khan lay down again.

"Where does your mother work?"

"In the Street of the Sirens."

"Who keeps the house?"

"He is called How Chin. He is from the east."

"A man called Bessus. Does he come to the house?"

A silent, affirmative nod from the huddled figure in the corner.

"And Hin Sho?"

"I never saw him! I swear I never saw him! My mother said, he will cut her face so no man will ever want her again, and we will starve."

Cephan raised the feeble lamp. The boy looked up, and though his face was marked by tears and terror, he was beautiful.

"So," Cephan said, "what shall I do with you now? I can give you to the king, and tell him how you tried to kill his horse - - -."

The thin, ragged figure at his feet shook with sobs.

"------- Or I can return you to Hin Sho and tell him how you gave his name to me - - -."

"I beg you, have mercy!"

Still holding the little lamp aloft, Cephan squatted beside his prisoner.

"You are young," he said softly, "but fate has willed that you must now become a man, and make your choices like a man. I am going to leave you here. Khan will be at the door, but that matters little to you, for you have no-where to run. If you go to your mother, you will be discovered, and she will suffer more. If you hide they will hunt you down like a rat in a cellar. If you flee the city, you will be caught by the king's horsemen. But I will leave you with this little bottle, so that you may choose your way."

Daylight disclosed death, and some of Abdullah's men found the body of the water-boy. He had been a small boy, and his death was a small death, a matter of lonely, agonised moments in the dark, with the glass phial in his twisted little fingers.

The king and his kingdom, his men and his horses, are now long since dust, but that small, thick cylinder of crazed glassware was found some ten years ago, when the site was open to the world, by archaeologists. It seemed to have been hidden in the masonry of the stables of the citadel, and it created a puzzle for the clever men who discovered it, for they knew that any form of glassware was prized in those far-off days, and chemists shook their heads over an analysis of the minute scrapings of its dried-out contents. Having been looted from the museum in the modern city, it was auctioned in Cairo and is now in the possession of a Japanese business man whose identity I cannot disclose.

CHAPTER 11

P armenion's farm, his place of pleasure, where he was as free as a tyrant may ever be from care, lay on the plain below the vast crag where stood his palace. Cephan was lodged in comfort, and the stallion was under armed guard day and night.

Phoebe was there, who had asked, grave faced, if she might come with him. He had looked at her sideways, but there had been no promise in her grey eyes. And because they had become, if not friends, then at least allies against the world, he had left it too late now to force her. In any case, if she was a spy, he did not need her in his bed. Now she came through the dawn shadow, muffled against the cold and with one slim hand at her throat to hold the folds of her head covering together. In the stable the grooms were asking, Did he want the mule led out with the horse?

"Yes", he said, "let them come together, and the mule should be tethered so he can graze."

He sipped cautiously at the bowl of thin, hot gruel she had brought him, and considered how many days he had left for his task. Not enough. Khan was lying at his cold feet, and he thrust them under the hound's recumbent body for warmth, making him grunt. Not nearly long enough.

Messiah came out boldly, barely restrained by two men, and Mule came ambling peaceably behind to be tethered where he could watch the proceedings and where, far more importantly, the stallion could see him.

Cephan took the two halter ropes and then dismissed the grooms, who scurried thankfully away.

"If you frighten men," he said softly to the horse, "they will find ways to defeat you, so as to wipe away their shame."

Messiah swung his massive head one way and the other, ears twitching, alert for the slightest movement, the smallest noise, then he whinnied at Mule, who paid no attention, and finally he seemed to settle a little.

"Here we are," said Cephan "so that I can sit upon your back, so you can be ridden as other horses are."

Messiah rolled a doubtful eye, gave a defiant snort.

"As other horses are," Cephan repeated calmly, looking at his height, which was greater than that of any horse he had ever sat on.

"Yesterday you carried a sack of maize on your back" he continued, talking softly, "and you did that very well - -."

Here an approving pat on the horse's neck.

"And now you can carry me, which is just as easy."

Cephan was calm, and methodical, and he moved slowly, step by unhurried step. By the time the morning was well advanced he was sitting in a makeshift saddle, riding Messiah about on the level sand, directing his progress with the halter ropes at a gentle walk. The grooms looked on and shook their heads in wonderment, and Mule went on grazing, and Khan, not so gaunt now after long days of palace living, slumbered in the shade. Phoebe, watching from the tent awning, noticed how the man's face had become rapt as he sat searching for union with the child-mind of the horse.

Enough for the day, and Cephan was confirmed in what he had already guessed, that the stallion was quick, and sharp, but also biddable, if bidden with courtesy and calm. What his reaction might be if treated otherwise, Cephan had no wish to discover.

He slid to the ground, which seemed not as far down as it had been when he mounted, and gave the horse a pat. Seeing the grooms approaching, he whispered, "I will come in the night time", before they led him, docile now as an old mare, to the stables.

The sun was far above the mountains, bleaching the heavens and parching the steppe. Phoebe had brought a ewer of water for his hands, and a napkin. Silently, she washed them, and he had a sudden memory of his old nurse doing the same, in another time and another country. He had washed his own hands in the years since then, but now, for a while, it seemed that the bones had rolled his way, and the living was soft, and easy. It would not be for long.

As he had promised, he came to the stables that night. The guard he courteously dismissed, telling them that his hound would serve as such so that they might rest. They were thankful to wrap their black cloaks about them and find their beds. Cephan had commanded men in his time, and he knew that a kind word was remembered when orders were long forgotten.

And Khan, of course, was no gossip, and would say nothing of his master's quiet visits to the stable at such hours.

Messiah was down in his clean sand with his legs tucked under his great bulk in the unlikely fashion that horses use. He remained couched, and simply pricked his ears as Cephan dragged aside the barrier and slipped like a shadow inside.

"So," said Cephan, "are you more content now? You have Mule down the line there, and I am here, and Khan is here to guard you."

He put out a hand, and stroked the horse's nose. Messiah extended his head, the white blaze down his face clear in the moonlight, and let his nostrils explore his visitor's chest. Cephan was encouraged to offer a kind word to a young horse.

"We began well, this morning," he said, "You see now, how easy is the work."

There followed a silence, in which Cephan realised his mistake.

"As it seems to me," Messiah replied, "I must learn to bear a burden, and carry it well. I must suffer as all my kind before me and after me."

"I hope," Cephan said stiffly, "that as a burden, I do not ask you to suffer too much."

"No," Messiah answered after a moment, "You have treated me well, and you are not a heavy man.

Cephan swallowed.

"You are very kind."

"And I know that you will not forsake me," Messiah continued. Rolled himself over, he thrust out his forelegs and heaved his bulk upright, shaking his great frame so that the sand flew from his coat.

"You may trust me in all things" said Cephan, stepping hastily backward.

"Because you have chosen your path and can find no other now." the stallion went on.

"Not so," Cephan said sharply, not liking to have his word discounted so casually. "For I could, if I wished, leave you to the mercies of the king."

"And go where? You and your hound, who is your only friend in all the world? You are old and sick, and soon you will die. How long before the fever takes you again? And when it does, what price a broken man to a king who needs a horse to keep a throne?"

Cephan was dumb, and Messiah made a noise in his nostrils that might have been laughter.

"For so it is, is it not? The king's heir must be the victor in the festival, or else lose the kingdom. And he must display himself, and be acclaimed, as was the great Alexander. On such a horse as I am."

Cephan remained silent.

"You forget," Messiah continued scornfully, "I was bred in the king's stables. Do you think I learned nothing with my mother's milk?"

"If you wish it, I can set you free." Cephan muttered.

"As you said before, on the road back to Sirika. So now, tell me about this young man, who wishes to ride me in triumph into Sirika. Is he brave enough? Will he be my master? Is he such a rider as you are? "

"He is the king's son, and his only heir. If he fails, the kingdom will pass to another, and Parmenion will die in the dark. As well he knows."

"All that I know too. But I am a horse, and I scorn birth, and the standing of a man. Tell me what concerns me."

"About my height and weight, and well made. He spends time in the gymnasium, and he carries himself. He is well-favoured."

"I care nothing for his face. Does he sit upon his horses in perfect poise, like a lance at rest? Does his hand on the rein make the weight of it sweet in the mouth? Shall I desire to dance beneath him?"

"He rides well enough." Cephan replied.

"Ah! I see! Well enough! And this young Well-Enough is to ride me in triumph to the gates of Sirika in how many days?"

"Eighty two." answered Cephan, affecting a nonchalance he was far from feeling.

"Really! Upon my word, some horses in my position would think you very impertinent."

And Messiah rolled a scornful eye, and Cephan remained silent.

"Where is Mule?" Messiah asked finally.

"Stalled with the other mules, as you know."

"I want him here. In the stable besides mine. You can get rid of that fat, pompous Arab gelding who screams with fright every time I look at him, and allow me one friend I can trust. After what you have just told me, it's the very least I expect."

It was the dead hour of the night. The night wind came exploring, and a fox yapped beyond the hill. Khan patrolled the shadows and then came searching for his master. Cephan went miserably away. His head had begun to ache and his body to sweat, and he knew what came next.

Cleitus at the parapet above the great North Gate, looked down the road across the plain with the sun going down, where the tents and camps of the early comers to the festival were set, and the drift of fire-smoke hardly moved in the still air. Peaceful enough, he thought, eying the horizon, seeing no flicker of the signal beacon at the outpost there.

And yet he felt that curious squeeze in his stomach that came with danger. For many days now he had watched men with their horses appear like ghosts over the steppe, and had gone out with patrols to chivvy them a safe distance from the walls and to ensure that there was water enough for all comers in the channels that were fed from the wells. There had been no trouble, but Cleitus had seen how his men had been studied, their bearing, their weapons and their armour. He had doubled the guard for the night watch, which now stood sentinel above the gate, four chosen men motionless besides their tall spears, bronze helmeted with shields at rest.

"If anything moves in those hills, or on that road, you sound the tocsin," he ordered. "There'll be no bad word from me if it's a stray donkey, but I'll have all four of you flogged if a mouse makes it to the gates unmarked. Remember Attila."

Attila was the mortally wounded spy whose mule had brought him home down the dark road some days ago. He had not been seen until he slipped in his own blood from the animals back onto the stones of the gateway, and the physician had said that had he been recovered earlier he might have spoken before he died.

"The watchword?"

"Oxhead"

The guard grounded the heavy butts of their spears in salute, and Cleitus turned away and descended the stone steps.

"Duty calls again," said one man as Cleitus disappeared. "The old dog!"

"She must be a tasty one," muttered another.

"Whatever, he's at her like a ram with the sheep," said the third, "Almost every night. You'd wonder where he keeps her."

Cleitus made his way up the narrow street toward the House of the Winds, between the shopkeepers who were closing their doors against the deepening shadows, jostled by loaded pack animals and their hasty keepers, and citizens afoot for home before the curfew horn. Here and there were the Chosen, instantly recognisable by their black cloaks, never alone and always armed, making now for the barracks in the citadel where safety lay. Not for many days had they ventured out at night at less than squadron strength.

At the palace gates waited Tosto, although Cleitus knew his way without that little figure scurrying ahead of him along the colonnade and so to the terrace where the king waited with his son.

They lay on their couches by the black-water pool with the lilies asleep in little green shells tilted sideways on a surface so still that the moon seemed to drown there. The night air was heavy with the scent of roses. All very peaceful, Cleitus thought as he made his stiff-legged way toward them.

Parmenion on his feet in time to answer the raised-fist salute with his own, with Mylon watching the exchange with a faint, a very faint smile as he remained undisturbed.

"Wine before words, between friends!" said Parmenion, and Tosto capered forward with his flagon, and Cleitus drank and wiped his lips on his leather sleeve, and sighed inwardly.

"Good news at last!" the king said. "That young cub Hephaestion heeds his father after all!"

Cleitus nodded.

"Indeed, sir. And he and his friends tell all who will listen in the taverns how his father heeded the king."

"A tall tale indeed! That I would meddle with a priest at such a time, when all must court the favour of the god. It would be sacrilege!"

"Aye, Sir. They say that such a king must fall."

Cleitus was standing like a dusty ghost at the limit of the torchlight, and his words were cold.

"I am not frightened of Hephaestion," Mylon said, "I should have defeated him."

He waved a hand dismissively.

"Are they believed, these young firebrands?" Parmenion asked.

"Some laugh at them, but some do not."

"Do not concern yourself, Sir," said Mylon, "Hephaestion and his friends are noisy in their cups. Sparks from the fire, no more."

Cleitus exchanged a glance with his king.

"Sparks indeed," Parmenion replied. "In a tinderbox of a city we need no sparks."

Mylon looked from one grave face to the other, then gave a small, exasperated shrug.

" And now I have against me only old Bessus, not a serious man, and Antheus, whose horse is dead lame."

"Behind Bessus stands Hin-Sho," Cleitus said heavily, "and men die who do not take him seriously."

But Mylon was looking at his reflection in the black mirror water of the pool.

"I think that I am well-liked in Sirika. And the priests will hear the voice of the people."

The older men regarded him silently, and Mylon smiled.

"Hin-Sho is a horse thief from the steppe," he said, "and he plays tricks, but that's all. He tried to have the stallion poisoned, and look where that got him."

"You forget," Cleitus replied grimly, "the lad who died by his own hand rather than go back. I passed his mother in the square as I came here. She was begging for bread and praying for death in the same breath. They say Hin-Sho gave her to his bodyguard for the night before he sliced off her nose and her ears. That's the man who plays tricks for you."

"Don't try to frighten me, Cleitus," Mylon said sulkily, "I am not a boy."

The king looked at his son.

It is a hard thing for a father to judge a son fairly and to accept his own verdict. Parmenion had long since understood that this dubious, unloved child was not the stuff of warriors, not a king to rule men or govern a fractious land. In the years gone by, while Mylon was but a youth, Parmenion had hoped that time would make this misbegotten son a man. But now there was no more time, and everything, even Parmenion's own life, depended on this pretty lad who now lay back on his couch and had told the old soldier who stood respectfully before him that he was not a boy. The old soldier, as Parmenion could clearly see, did not believe him.

"I mean no disrespect, Sir," Cleitus said, with the faintest emphasis on the "sir", "but you must see that it is Hin-Sho, not Bessus, that you must defeat in the contest, Likewise, it is not Antheus but his father who gambles everything he has for the kingdom."

"Everything?" Parmenion asked.

"Where money may be spent, he spends it, Sir."

"Antheus's horse is lame," Mylon repeated petulantly.

"And I've heard that Sorbon has bought him another," Cleitus replied. "From beyond Tartary, some say from the stables of the emperor himself. A beautiful grey mare, trained to bridle on a silken thread, and it moves like a dancing girl."

Mylon sniggered.

"She won't be dancing with Antheus on her back!"

But Parmenion was suddenly staring at Cleitus.

"From beyond Tartary? From the emperor? With no report from the eastern border and not a patrol returned. One spy dead, and another missing. And Sorbon buys a horse there fifty days before the festival! How is this?"

"I can't tell you that, Sir." Cleitus replied woodenly.

"I should have been told of this, Cleitus. There have been no traders from the east these four moons Not one."

"Have Sorbon arrested," Mylon said languidly, "and have him questioned in the place beneath. He'll tell us soon enough."

And this, Parmenion thought bitterly, is the boy in whom the fate of Sirika might be entrusted! He caught Cleitus's eye, and his old companion looked away.

"You well know," Parmenion replied, "that entrants at the festival are sacred, from the moment it is declared until the new king is hailed. I cannot touch Antheus, or anything that belongs to him. Least of all his own father!"

Mylon shrugged, and looked sulkily into the pool.

. "And you have known this too, since you were a boy! Once the contest is called, the ruling king acts only to defend Sirika. All else is unlawful."

"The arrest of a traitor?" Cleitus suggested.

"On what evidence? That he bought a horse for his son? He would laugh in my face."

Parmenion's voice was suddenly very tired, and his face was haggard. With an effort he pulled back his shoulders and seemed to remember that he was indeed a king.

"Mazares, with his mercenaries, must march east" he said grimly. "And from the city - ."

He stood lost in thought, considering his available strength.

"Five hundred of the Chosen" he said finally.

Cleitus stiffened but said nothing. He was a soldier.

Mylon gasped.

"And leave only one regiment for our defence, if there is insurrection!"

That, of course, was the silent fear of the Chosen at the time of the festival, when all was for the taking in the city, and a noisy, unruly throng caroused and quarrelled the day into the night. If the Chosen ever lost control of the city, went the accepted wisdom, then Sirika would burn. And yet now Parmenion was ordering half of his crack troops, the black-cloaked fighting men whose loyalty was unquestioned, to march out of the city.

"They are garrisoned in Sirika presently, Sir" Cleitus said at last, "Men will mark their going."

"Thank you, Cleitus! Always a wise friend. But it must be so. That will be all."

Cleitus raised his fist in salute, then turned away.

"And Cleitus."

"Sir?"

"The wine in the guard-house now. Is it fit for drinking?"

Cleitus smiled, and for a sweet moment the two men were comrades once more.

"Indeed it is, Sir. No complaints."

CHAPTER 12

We call it malaria nowadays. The Victorians who encountered the mosquito-borne virus dosed themselves with quinine and shivered and sweated in their tents until it abated or, equally likely, killed them.

For Cephan, no such relief. The night ran into the dawn, and the dawn became an interminable day of heat and cold, and he was too confused to care whether he lived or died. Khan was there, by his mattress, to guard him, as was the king's steward who was just as concerned that his charge should recover, if for different reasons. On the third day, Cephan saw a bearded face over his own, with Phoebe hovering behind with a potion that her mother, who had been a queen, had made in the days of her childhood.

"Is that you, Ashwin? Yes, I see it is. You need not look so worried, my friend. Your skin is safe, for the moment at least. I'm not going to die."

He propped himself on his elbow and drank the steaming liquid that the girl offered him.

"How it burns! But perhaps I am better at last."

Phoebe smiled slightly, and left him. Cephan's bleary gaze followed the slim sway of her body, and he sighed.

"That's a remedy that would cure a man of his ills, Ashwin," he muttered and then,

"How many days this time?"

"Three days and four nights, lord. The king himself will rejoice in your recovery. He has sent daily for news."

"And the stallion?"

"We have been able to tend him most carefully, lord. The great hound has been with you, so there have been problems with him here, but in the stables no difficulty, only - - -."

Ashwin's wizened countenance twisted ruefully.

"He got out, lord. The stable boys, they say he is too great for his confinement in such a space. And so he - - departed, lord."

Cephan jerked himself upright, became suddenly dizzy, and sank back.

"He got out!"

"Sadly, lord, yes. He kicked out the door. And then when we chased after him he turned on us as if we were rats from the cellar."

"May the gods deliver me! And then?"

"He tired, lord. And the mule which by your order is next to him in the stables began to bray like a trumpet, and he heard it and he went back to his place. A most remarkable animal, lord."

"Is he injured?"

"On my life, not a scratch on his hide."

"And Khan here?"

"Has not left your side since you fell into the sickness, as I said. There have been - - ."

Ashwin looked bitterly at the hound, who let his tongue loll from his jaws as he looked calmly back.

"Difficulties."

"Well," Cephan said, "he must be fed. Away with you, Khan my friend, and follow this man. He will give you a sweet kid, presently."

Ashwin swallowed nervously as the great hound stretched himself.

"There is another small matter."

"Indeed?"

"There is a falcon, lord. A grey-backed falcon with her wings as white as winter beneath, and she sits on the roof above - - ."

Ashwin pointed.

"She has not moved since we saw her sitting there in the morning two days ago. One of the mule boys said she was a bird trained to hunt and would come to him if she hungered."

"And?" Cephan asked, with that lop-sided grin that lifted several days beard like a hank of black hemp.

"He climbed up to her with meat he had stolen from my stores. She let him get very close, and then she struck him with her talons and ripped his face open!"

"Ah!" said Cephan, "She is a fine bird indeed!"

When Ashwin was gone, he limped out to look. There she was, affecting not to notice him, preening her plumage in the morning light like a left over angel.

"What brings you to visit me on my bed of sickness, Phaedra?" he asked.

She restored a pinion of one wing to its rightful place with her beak, roused all her feathers and looked down at him.

"I spied you with the golden horse below me, and I came a-looking."

He raised his fist, and she came gracefully down on half-open wings.

"Still in the king's good graces, I see" she said, "but for how much longer, I wonder?"

"So do I wonder, Phaedra," he replied, "for I must alloy yonder golden horse with a base-metal rider, who is the king's son."

"You talk in riddles!" she said crossly.

"Forgive me, Lady. The answer is, 'not long'."

"No," she replied, staring at him yellow-eyed and malevolent, "not long at all. For two dawns since, I was far to the east of here, and I spied a marching host of warriors. They come to take Sirika, and the ravens and the crows, and the base-born who feed on carrion flesh, follow gladly behind. They come slowly, with so many to feed and water, but nothing stands in their way. Now they camp by the river, two days' march from Sirika."

"The king sends no force against him?"

"The king knows nothing, as I guess, for there are two squadrons whose bodies feed the foxes where they died around their standards in the hills. His enemy keeps the king in darkness!"

"He is earthbound, like all mankind, my sweet Phaedra."

"Sweet nothing! But yes, I grant you, he is but a creature of the dust."

She examined the talons of one claw complacently.

"So," he said softly, "the emperor's men march for Sirika while all wait upon the festival, and Parmenion must keep the city safe while his rivals play for his throne, and plot against him."

"When I was young," Phaedra mused, "I had a rival in the nest for the food our parents brought. It was a hard year, and there was not enough. So, I killed my rival before it killed me. Why cannot your king do the same?"

"Ah," Cephan said, rocking her up and down on his fist in the way she enjoyed, "There's the worst of it. For the festival is declared in the name of the god, who might favour his choice and so make his wish known. Therefore, all who contend for the kingdom are sacred and must not be harmed."

"Gently! Not so rough!"

Phaedra fanned her wings wide against the sky, stretching upward.

"The ways of men!" she cried, "How I rejoice that I am of the sky-born kindred! As I know by the wind that carries me and the sun that lights my way, that there are no gods, save in your foolish dreams! And so, farewell!"

She lifted her wings, and was in a moment wheeling upward in the still blue morning air.

The horse's body was balanced so perfectly over his legs that their movement seemed as inevitable as the cadence of a song. With every stride came a soft exhalation from his wide nostrils. Cephan sat quietly in the saddle, absorbed in the power beneath him with his hand gentle on the rein, but the stallion saw before he did the arrival of the king's squadron and promptly spoiled this picture of perfect harmony with a shy and a buck that would have unseated almost any other rider.

Cephan regained control, brought the excited stallion toward the newcomers, and gave him a pat when he consented to stand before them. Not the heavy slap on the neck with which so many riders reward their steeds but a soft scratch of his fingers there, just above the wither, where you will see horses at pasture nibble each other of an afternoon.

Then he slid to the ground, and the waiting slave came to lead away the stallion, his bright coat dark with sweat and his lips white with the telltale foam that a horse makes in his mouth only when he is happy with his rider's hand.

And so we have our man, our ragged, whip-thin man, stood erect and alone before King Parmenion and his son, who sat on their horses above him on the dry sand.

"We would have wished to see more," the king said.

"I ride before the heat of the day, lord, and the horse has worked well. Your coming disturbed him, but then he stood before you, which was a good lesson for him. And so we finish as friends after a march. It is enough."

Parmenion looked down from his saddle.

"My son, Prince Mylon, will ride the horse when we are rested."

Prince Mylon, now afoot, was of a height with the horse master, and the open, smiling gaze of the one was at a level with the dark stare of the other. So it is that age meets youth, and bitterly understands how it cannot prevail.

"So, Horsemaster, you made good your boast that night when you came to my father's hall! Come with me, and you shall tell me all about this horse. Already he is a creature from a legend!"

Ashwin hovered, directed, saw the two men seated on soft cushions, and clapped his hands and shouted that wine and water must be brought directly.

Phoebe did no more than stand with the morning behind her, and an earthenware ewer on her hip. She wore only the humble, white muslin shift of the slaves, but in some way she had tucked its folds close about her body. Her blond hair had been caught in simple wooden combs at the nape of her neck, and so her proud, perfect beauty had no setting, and plainly needed none.

She looked calmly, grey-eyed, down at the two men seated before her. To Cephan she bowed her head. Then she saw Mylon, and she smiled.

"If you wish for beauty," said the looking-glass to the virgin, "you have only to smile." However that may be, Phoebe smiled, and Mylon's heart thudded in his chest, and he felt the blood rise to his cheeks. Prince Mylon, contender for the throne of Sirika, son of a reigning king, caught in the net of a slave girl!

Cephan saw nothing. Sensitive to the hair-trigger reactions of a horse, capable of divining the flight of a falcon, watchful for every need of his great hound, he missed what happened under his nose.

The tableau was over in a moment. Ashwin scolded the girl for her indolence, the ewer was placed carefully down, and Phoebe was gone.

Passion comes like a sudden storm, and takes a man unawares. Unaccountably, his heart throbs loud in his chest, and his breath comes short. His mind is a whirl of unbidden thoughts, and he controls it only with difficulty, as Mylon did now, looking sideways at Cephan and setting himself to be agreeable to his strange companion.

"A fine stallion indeed, my father has bred. I shall see how he suits me."

Had he not ridden horses since he was a child and been a cavalryman since his youth? Had he not ridden out on campaign, and seen action, and killed his man? This wizened old sceptre with his horrid scar and his terrible hound need not tell him how to ride a horse.

Cephan looked at him speculatively.

"I will help you, prince. If I can."

Mylon smiled.

"I can manage the horse," he replied, "for I saw how easily he went for you."

"He has a soft mouth," Cephan persisted, "so you must be careful of that."

"They say in Sirika that I have a good hand with a horse" said Mylon with a confident smile.

That is because you are a prince, Cephan thought sadly.

"It would be better, if you tried him tomorrow, Sir. He needs rest, like any other, and the sun is high now. If you could persuade your father the king - - ."

The young man laughed.

"Persuade my father! I can but try, Horsemaster, if you are so anxious for your charge, but he will say, 'First light and not a moment later'. He has cares awaiting him in the city."

Daybreak, and the camp not yet astir, but two slaves leading the stallion from the stable to his training ground. He jogged restlessly, and the men had to trot beside him. Cephan came to take the horse, and then rode off across the sand.

"Now," he said softly, "today we do a different thing. You are to be ridden by another."

"Aha!" the stallion replied, "I guessed as much! Young Well Enough is it?"

"Indeed so. I pray you, treat him tenderly, so he can ride you at the festival and so be glorified."

" I can move only so well for him as he can ride me," Messiah replied with a toss of his golden mane. "No horse can do more, even one such as I am."

"I know it," Cephan said softly. Over by the entrance to the arena King Parmenion sat on his horse with his escort about him.

"But at the least, you will give him a fair trial? You will be patient with him?"

Of course no horse can give such an undertaking, as Cephan well knew, and Messiah gave a derisive snort.

Mylon came out yawning, paused to take in the morning and the great animal moving brightly before him like a jewel on pale silks, and then he smiled as only young men smile, a smile of pure well-being.

"Well met!" he exclaimed. "Even so early, and I scarce warmed my bed last night!"

Cephan slipped down from Messiah, answering Mylon's smile with a sour grimace.

"Your father waits to go."

"No matter," the young man said gaily, "on such a morning as this!"

Messiah was looking about, had seen the stir of men about the arena, had realised that any mischief of his would be noticed. He arched his neck proudly, and Cephan saw that the signal went unmarked.

"Remember, Sir. Be careful of his mouth."

"Dear old Horsemaster, do not concern yourself! I shall not hurt your precious stallion."

"I am not concerned for the horse," Cephan replied, "I am concerned for you, Sir. I would not wish you to be harmed."

Mylon laughed, hopped up into the saddle easily enough, and Cephan let go of Messiah's bridle.

"Gently," he muttered to the horse, "for my sake if not your own!"

But Messiah had no care for consequences, no desire to please this stranger on his back. As he had said, he would go as well as he was ridden, no more and no less.

Mylon, as became a prince, was no mean horseman. Only Cephan could see that he sat slightly to one side and that Messiah moved his quarters underneath the greater weight there, and after a few moments began to lean on his rider's hand so as to balance himself. Nonetheless he made a picture worth looking at, and there was a murmur of approval from the men who had gathered to watch. Messiah looked at them sideways as he cantered past, and his banner of a tail began to switch in warning.

Cephan waited. He knew that all horses go more easily to one side or the other and that Messiah was now on his better rein, taking Mylon's imperfect balance in his stride with the slightly greater weight under the left side of his body. But now the prince brought the horse to circle before his audience, and Messiah set his jaw against the increased pressure of the bronze bit in one side of his mouth as he came, obediently enough, into the manoeuvre. His tail switched again, and Cephan knew what would happen next, as did the watching Parmenion, who also understood the meaning of that uneasy tail.

Nothing has changed. Men ride horses, and do it well or badly in the same ways.

For Mylon now thought to move out of his circle and to change his rein. In other words the horse, so far carrying his rider well enough, had to change to his weaker side while his rider's balance remained askew and so hindered him.

And he tried. In his equine way the horse did his best. Cephan, watching, thought for a moment that all might be well. But in his effort Messiah had to bear on that unlevel contact in his mouth, and Mylon sought to correct this with a hearty yank of his right hand.

The rider has not yet been born who can sit on a horse who wishes in good earnest to throw him. A rodeo cowboy is lucky to stay in the saddle for more than ten seconds. Cephan himself could not have sat on the enraged stallion's huge, twisting buck as he wrenched the reins from Mylon's fist and buried his head between his knees. The prince was launched into the air and then came crashing to the sand, where he lay still. Messiah galloped off and then began to graze the withered grass at the side of the arena. There was a rush of men, with Ashwin yelling orders and the slaves in confusion.. King Parmenion, still sitting on his horse, spoke quietly to one of his escort and then turned for the road to Sirika.

Cephan saw him go, and then watched as Mylon was carried away. He knew now that Parmenion's son would never ride Messiah for the throne of Sirika, and he knew that the king knew it too. He walked over to the horse, took the trailing reins, and led him back to his stable. He felt weak and a little dizzy, because of the fever, he told himself, and he put up one hand to the horse's shoulder to steady himself. Into the other was thrust a wet muzzle, and there was Khan, pushing his body against his master's legs to support him.

"So," Cephan whispered as the slaves came running, "Well Enough was not well enough after all."

"No," Messiah agreed calmly, "and I never thought he would be, from the moment he sat on my back."

There was no Phoebe to help Cephan to his mattress, only a kitchen boy who brought him water. He huddled under his blankets, eyeing the bright morning as it came to life with a sense of detachment, a little bemused by the colours of the day.

The light was fading before anyone came. Khan lay beside him and frightened the boy who hovered in the entrance with the water jug. In his lucid moments Cephan tried to guess at the future but without success, and he did not much care. He was drifting in a nightmare when he heard his name called, and Khan girning, afoot beside the mattress with his tail lashing. Ashwin was standing at the door.

"Prince Mylon has sent me to fetch you to his presence."

The slaves came with basins and sponges, and Cephan was grateful for the water on his hot skin. They took away his blankets and they dressed him as if he were a child. Then, supporting him on either side and with Khan pacing behind, they brought him before the prince.

Mylon was pale, and he lay on a bed of snowy coverings, propped up by richly worked cushions. Beside him, bearing a silver bowl of warm water perfumed with roses, stood Phoebe.

Mylon smiled wanly at his visitor.

"Come closer, Horsemaster," he said "for I owe you some words of apology."

"The girl is not mine, sir," Cephan responded wearily. "She belongs to your father's household."

The young man's laughter was succeeded by a cry of pain.

"Oof! How my ribs hurt me! No, Horsemaster, not the girl! I well know that my father offered her to you. But she came when she saw my fall, being skilful in remedies, and indeed her dressing has eased my pain. She has such soft hands too. Do you not, Phoebe?"

He twisted his body to look up at her, and she shook her head and smiled.

"Be still, Lord," she said in that harsh, broken voice, "or you will not mend."

"Well, but you must serve our friend here, as my father ordered. Go with him now. He will forgive your care of me, will you not, Horsemaster?"

Phoebe looked across at Cephan, and her look was one of gratitude, and a strange pity.

"He has been kind to me," she said, "No man ever treated me so well."

Ashwin tutted furiously, thinking such an avowal from a slave-girl unseemly. The two guards at the entrance exchanged glances of astonishment. Mylon was suddenly solicitous of the thin figure before him, still held upright by the slaves.

"Let him down beside the bed. Gently there! Put the cushions so! Phoebe, you must bathe his face with your marvellous water."

But Cephan warded her off.

"I am well enough, sir. I have no need of the girl."

"Then send her away now, if you please. And Ashwin, off you go. Let the guard go with you. No, Ashwin you fool! The man carries no weapon, as you can well see!"

And so they were alone together, the injured contender for the throne of Sirika and the ill, feverish horse master, now lying uneasily beside him on piled cushions.

"I wanted to say I should have listened," said Mylon "I should have behaved as gently to your stallion as you have behaved to Phoebe, it seems."

As near as a prince may go to thank a vagrant horseman for his forbearance to a palace girl, but Cephan understood only his literal meaning.

"Women and horses, sir, are very much the same. Gentleness and patience are the keys that unlock their doors."

The young man hesitated for a moment.

"Did my father speak to you before he rode away?"

"No, Sir."

"He will think I cannot ride the horse."

Poor prince! Flattery from courtiers all his life, and endless praise from palace riders to plaster the cracks of his self-esteem!

But Cephan held his tongue. Khan laid his great, shaggy bulk down beside him, and Cephan dragged with one hand at the hound's ragged ear.

"I never sat on such a horse," Mylon continued, "I shall ride him better, another day."

Ill as he was, Cephan could see what was required of him, and he knew he could not tell the prince what he wanted to hear. He could lie as well as the next man, and had done so shamelessly when necessity arose all his life. But in this one thing he could only tell the truth.

"The days are not many now before the festival, Sir. There are ten days, and you must keep your bed a while."

Mylon twisted toward the thin figure beside him.

"You must tell me," he insisted, "for if I cannot - - -."

Cephan lay silently.

"You must tell me," Mylon repeated.

Cephan sighed wearily.

"The horse told you," he replied, "As horses always will."

He was looking sideways at his tormentor. Only a boy, he thought sadly, to be told such a hard thing.

The prince lay back with a sigh.

"Yes," he said, "and I have had many such messages. How the gods play with us, old man! You have nothing in the world, but you ride that horse like - Like a prince! And me, he throws in the sand like a beggar."

"There are better things than horses," Cephan replied softly. "It is no great matter, how a man rides his horse."

Mylon gave a little, bitter cough.

"Not so, old man! And certainly not so now! If I could ride like you, I would come away from the festival as a king! Oh yes! It is a great matter indeed how a man rides a horse!"

Cephan said nothing. He wished only to be left in peace, to sweat out his fever. He closed his eyes wearily, and Mylon, seeing this, muttered to himself, letting his thoughts come unhindered to his lips.

"Was there ever such a hopeless game as this? And now I must go before my father the king and bear his scorn and play favourite to the mob of the city and try for a throne I never wanted! And for what?"

Cephan stirred.

"Because if you do not, your father's enemies will rend him like a hunted hare."

He cast aside his cushions and staggered to his feet.

"If you will forgive me, Sir. You must rest, and I must wait out this cursed fever - - ."

At the entrance he turned, with thin fingers on Khan's neck, a spectral figure with the morning behind him.

"Heed my words, Sir," he said. "Prince may come to their kingdoms. Horsemen find only unmarked graves."

CHAPTER 13

P armenion drew rein at the brow of the last rise of the land, and his eyes traversed the scene before him while his escort sat their horses behind him and waited.

Peaceful, it seemed. From the great gate a to-and-fro like bees from a hive, and on the walls above the tiny figures of the duty guard and sharp lights as the evening sun caught the blades of their spears. There was a haze of wood smoke from innumerable cooking fires but not the angry, red-hearted belch of a house a-blaze or a riot. The tall arcades of the palace stood white beneath the sky, and at the very height of the city was the temple, alone on its high rock. Parmenion could just make out the paved road that ran there from his palace. He would be there, in the temple, before the day's end, to do his sacred duty. Or play his part in a game, he thought bitterly as he spurred his horse onward.

Beneath the great arch where the stone horses reared above the massive gates and the guard brought the butts of their spears crashing down in salute, Parmenion, although he had his escort close behind him, felt the skin on his back shiver as he rode up the narrow way that led to his palace. To either side of him men drew aside readily enough, and he stared straight ahead of him, as a king must, and seemed not to study the faces that looked up toward his own. No curses shouted from the crowd, no sullen looks. Nor smiles, nor calls of welcome either. All very quiet, very peaceful, and Parmenion not a whit deceived. He knew that his authority withered with each passing hour.

Later, in the hallowed shade of the temple, standing before the sacred stone, dusty and tired after his day in the saddle, he waited until Cairphas, the priest, brought forth the ancient slate upon which there were now ninety-two marks, and he made one more. Seven days before the festival commenced, before his power ran out like sand in a glass. And still no word from the eastern frontier.

He handed back the slate, muttered the customary phrases, and saw how the blue-veined old hands that received it trembled. He wanted to look up, to exchange a smile of fellowship, but he was ashamed, and he knew that Cairphas also was ashamed.

For Parmenion had made his deal with the high priest. It had been a slow, tortuous business, begun with wistful speculation that crystallized into deniable proposals and ended in a brisk bout of hard-nosed bargaining. As a result, Cairphas was now the owner of certain well-watered and fertile lands, and his son Hephaestion was no longer an aspirant for the throne of Sirika.

And so the old king and the old priest were bound together by their own conspiracy, each doomed in the estimation of the other by their private disgrace. So that

Parmenion stared down at the marble flags at his feet while Cairphas turned silently away with downcast eyes, and both men knew that the days of their friendship were gone.

It saddened Parmenion, as he waited while the white-gowned priest shuffled away with his acolytes in attendance, but he shrugged the feeling away. A man should shoulder the burden of his own sin and if Cairphas could not do as much, then so much the worse for him. If he repented of the bargain he had made, then he could throw himself at the feet of his god and ask for mercy. Parmenion had no such advantage,and neither did he seek it. Far better had been his sole guiding principle, to rely on cunning and the exercise of brutal and sudden force. So his secret deal with Cairphas entailed only this one regret, that by it he had lost a friend.

And yet, alone in the silent, cold shades of the temple, Parmenion felt somehow compelled to remain there, before the huge, flat slab of polished marble in which four irregular, crescent-shaped marks seemed to have been gouged from the surface, left by the hooves of the horse god as he bounded from the earth to which he would return to rule again.

Did he pray despite himself, unbeliever though he was, as he stood there? In his heart did he not ask forgiveness, strive to ease his dark soul, plead for mercy when the reckoning came? Men like Parmenion can never know the comfort of faith, but in moments such as this, taken unaware when they sense the presence of the listening god, Oh yes my friend, they pray indeed. Not like saints, fluent in their hopes and confessions, but awkwardly and half-ashamed, throwing down thoughts full of self-mockery and doubt. Let us hope that Hippon listened to the stricken king.

For Parmenion saw clearly now what he had so desperately attempted to conceal from himself. That morning, watching a clumsy boy trying to ride that mighty stallion, he had seen not a king in waiting but a pretender to a throne. All the road home he had nursed the bitter truth, sitting straight as a lance in his saddle with his face like a graven image, and unbidden yet again came the weary, years-old question. Who had sired such a son? Now, in solitude at last, unseen by men, his shoulders sagged and his features seemed moulded in a soft, grey clay of despair.

Then the heavy slapping of feet in the precinct gave warning, and when Nooran the chamberlain came running he saw his king turn from the altar in regal disbelief that he should have been so disturbed in that sacred place.

"News from Tartary, Lord! From beyond Tartary, indeed! For the emperor sends his envoy to wait upon you."

Zhang Qian had returned once more.

In previous years the envoy had come as a merchant and a diplomat both, and had entered the city by the main gate, as became a man of peace. This year, with an escort of two hundred cavalry, he made camp openly a little way from the wells where he could see the fortress, topped by the palace and the temple above, rise on its sudden cliffs. He had left five thousand men by the river some two days' march behind him.

He was a thin man, of frugal habits, but well attended and well furnished against the evening chill. He sat under an awning on soft cushions to ease his body after another long ride and sipped his tea. There he received Nooran, the king's chamberlain, sent with two heavily laden mules in the care of a slave, bearing gifts of welcome. There was fresh fruit, -- melons and pomegranates, oranges and grapes -, and flagons of crystal -clean water, cold from the royal cisterns, and sacks of grain for man and beast. The envoy was sincerely grateful, and he said so.

Nooran bowed.

"All I desire," said Zhang Qian, "is the company of a gentleman, to enjoy the feast my cook can now prepare."

He extended a graceful arm, bidding Nooran to recline with him. The chamberlain flushed with pleasure, but hesitated.

"I pray you, do not disdain my poor hospitality," the envoy murmured, "for I so crave the company of a like-minded man after so many days among - - well, soldiers and their kind. All good men - - , but - -, shall we say - - ,limited? I know you understand me."

Nooran needed no further encouragement, or much prompting during the intimate repast that followed, where the envoy's own wines were offered for the chamberlain's enjoyment. He spoke feelingly of the work that the festival entailed, how so much was laid upon his shoulders that he really believed that without his efforts there could be no festival at all. How it was that the king's own son was the favourite to win the crown, the golden horse having now been recovered - - - -.

"Tell me," Zhang Qian said softly, "about this horse."

It seems to be the case throughout the ages, that the less a man knows about horses, the more he has to say on the subject. Certainly Nooran expressed with conviction his opinion that no such animal had ever before trod the earth, that the king's son was now so sure of the crown that - - - .

Here he paused, suddenly recalling where his allegiance lay.

"I will say no more" he finished.

"Come," the envoy said, "Secrets are the enemies of true friendship."

He smiled, his face like a parchment mask and his eyes like black stones, and yet somehow it was a charming smile. He was, after all, a courtier.

"Well," Nooran replied, "I know I can trust your discretion. It is said in the city, and in the very palace, that the king makes a mockery of the games, and that he has so moved the odds in favour of his own son that he risks the anger of our god upon him. I only repeat what is said, and for your ears alone, you understand."

"Of course" said Zhang Qian, "A little more wine, for the night is mild, and there's a good moon to show you home again."

It so happened, that one of the baggage mules to carry the king's gifts to the envoy was our friend, Mule, and he, together with his fellows, found himself offloaded and left in the envoy's lines to await the chamberlain's return. He found himself tethered next to a superior white mule. Such animals, then as now, are very rare.

"I don't think we've met" said Mule at last, politely.

"I'm sure we haven't," the other replied, "for I come from the stables of the emperor himself."

"Ah," said Mule, "well, that explains it. I hope you have not found your march a long one."

"I carry the emperor's envoy," the white one answered, "and he is not a heavy man."

"And you may rest here a while, I suppose?"

"I don't expect to be here long. I shall be taken up to the palace, where I shall be better suited than I am to these conditions.".

In the dark, Mule's long ears twitched.

"Really," he said, "I don't think so. Only the king's horses stand there."

He was a wise one, that mule, offering just enough doubt to draw contradiction but not so much as to arouse hostility. The white one rose unsuspecting to the bait.

"Not for long now, they won't," he grunted. "My master comes to offer terms for surrender. If the king says no, then my master's catspaw will sweep the board."

"And who might he be, this - , ah, – catspaw?"

But the other had spied the ox-head brand on Mule's rump, and was suddenly suspicious.

"I really should not discuss matters of state with strangers" he said loftily.

"Ah," Mule replied, "we need not be as discreet as our masters. I see that you are a mule of the highest rank, and I am a poor creature of the baggage train, but we are both merely onlookers to whatever might unfold. With great respect, of course."

We all like to murmur confidentially in a private ear, and mules are no different from the rest of us. For a while the white mule was silent. Then finally he spoke.

"Between you and me - - ."

"Oh," Mule answered softly, "of course. Strictly in confidence."

"There is a merchant there who puts forward his son in a contest for the kingdom of Sirika. He has men going about the city to tell all who will listen that the contest is a fraud which it is, because the king's own son will ride the golden stallion all the world speaks of with bated breath, the one they call the Messiah. I ask you, how can there be games with my master waiting at the gates? Which is why our merchant has a gang of thugs ready to open them and overcome the guard, and welcome my master at the head of five thousand men. With such a force he can take the palace by storm and dispatch the new king and the old one together."

"And the Chosen?" asked Mule, "What will they say of this?"

"They know there has been falsehood, and that no good can come of it. They will not fight for a lost cause."

"And your master the envoy. What reward does he take away?"

"The treasury, for his men who have marched so far and will not otherwise be satisfied. But they will leave the women and the girls unmolested. It is agreed so."

"It surprises me a little," Mule said casually "that the emperor should trouble with a land so far away from his own."

"He sends men to the corners of the earth for horses. Always he struggles to maintain his borders against barbarian invaders, and his cavalry plead with him for better horses. And the emperor knows that the horses of the Fergana valley, bred in great numbers here, are the best. As horses go."

The white one snorted disdainfully.

"And he pays with silk" he continued, "The heavenly secret, the shining cloth. So that the trails of his baggage animals are called now, the Silk Roads! To buy horses!"

The white mule pulled at his forage morosely, and went on,

"And these nags that he sends for now, just because they come from the Fergana valley? Like all the rest of them, I shouldn't wonder! If there's rock to fall over, they will find it. If the grazing is suspect, they will gorge on it, and if the water is brackish they would rather die of thirst. And I've yet to meet one that could carry a load and be sound at the end of the day."

"I've heard," Mule said, "that they can go many days without water, far longer than the rest of us. Except the camels, of course."

"Poppycock!."

"And the golden stallion?" Mule enquired as if by afterthought, "that horse belonging to the old king. What becomes of him?"

"He is destined to be an emperor's darling, if they can get him home."

When finally, by a full moon, Nooran rcturned to the city, Mule was lucky. He carried neither the chamberlain's unsteady weight nor the bolts of silk that were the envoy's gift to the king.

CHAPTER 14

Phaedra had come unseen from the morning sky like a conjuror's revelation, appearing open-winged on the branch of the tree where she settled for a moment and then hopped down to where Cephan rested in its shade. In the courtyard the baggage animals were being loaded, with Ashwin yelling at the slaves and the escort lounging by their horses.

She cocked her head and scratched thoughtfully with one hind claw behind her ear, looking down at him. Khan growled.

"Well!" she said, "The tale I have to tell!"

Cephan held his wrist below her breast, and from her snowy plumage peeped the dreadful cluster of her hanging talons, which she then extended, taking his arm as delicately as a lady takes her escort's offered elbow. Then she settled again and her cold eyes considered him.

"Your time is measured," she said confidingly. "Your stillness will come, and your body will swell in the sun until it bursts, and you will be carrion."

Khan flattened his ragged ears against his skull.

"Heed her not," he panted, his tongue lolling. "She is little more than a chicken. She has no gift of seeing, before time makes all things plain."

"Right enough, you dusty old cur! But I am a hunter, and I seek weakness, the lame and the starved and the ancient, and I need no gift of seeing!"

Cephan coughed.

"Well," he said, "many thanks for that, Phaedra my sweet! But to your tale, which you came to tell."

He rocked the falcon on his fist in the way she liked.

"Now," he said again, coaxingly, "To your tale?"

"More gently! Well then, in the dawn light I came over Sirika, where there is a great gathering of men - - -."

"The festival," yawned Khan, "as is well known."

"And because I was high in the heavens, and not limping in the dust like yonder cur, I saw the first rays of the sun strike the white stones of the temple, where it stands on the height of the city and looks down on the plain, above the tall cliff where the black swifts race for flies and the martins nest there."

Phaedra paused for effect.

"And I saw a man come from the temple alone, and go to climb on the stone parapet at the cliff's edge. He was an old man, moving stiffly, and I saw the gold ring on his finger glint in the new light. He looked up, and saw me lifting on my wings above him. Then he raised his arms as if he too might fly, and cast himself from the rock. His white gown blew about his body as he fell, and I saw how his skull broke open like an egg, and the grey yoke splashed on the rocks far below."

Khan yawned again to show his disinterest.

"I never yet saw a man fly." Phaedra said smugly.

"Fate falls on Sirika," Cephan said heavily, "and the king. The festival called, and a horse that will not carry his son. Then comes an army camped by the river. And then a priest casts himself from the temple rock. What an augury is there!"

In the following centuries, the king's farm fell into ruin. There was a well, but sometimes it was dry, and there was little natural shade. Travellers wondered at first about the arena, with its surrounding stones, but the thin grass took hold soon enough, and the scrub followed, and the place reverted to nature. Then, in this century of ours, the road came like a concrete snake where the trail had been and bore the traffic that brought the tourists to Sirika and beyond, and the heavy lorries. In the recent war, it brought the tanks and the armoured cars of the present day rivals for power. You can see some of the burnt-out wrecks in the ditches still. An enterprising Afghan who had been to America thought the place ideally suited for a road side cafe and paid the necessary bribes to enable him to build one. It flourished for a few years, as the surrounding litter of Coke cans and plastic will show, and the place where two men stood with a horse in that long-ago dawn is now the concrete floor of what was the ladies lavatory.

Cephan returned to a city beset by rumours where the air was heavy with foreboding. In the ravine below the temple rock, men were still trying to recover the body of the chief priest, and onlookers watched the flickering light of their torches from the city walls. Hephaestion stood with his friends apart, and there was muttering of murder. Parmenion had sent guards of the Chosen to the houses of Bessus, Hin-Sho, and Sorbon and his son, - for their own protection, as he said, - in such numbers that they could face down the surly mobs that gathered there. And the festival? Nobody knew, and the host that was now camped outside the walls of Sirika sat about their fires and met at the wells, and waited.

In the hour after dawn the following day, a little later than was customary, men saw the king go up to the temple with his duty guard in good order about him, and wait before the altar for the slate to be brought, so he could make the ritual mark upon it. And brought it was, by the newly elected head of the priesthood of Hippon, a former acolyte of the unfortunate Cairphas who had so tragically fallen to his death when overcome by an ecstasy the previous morning. He was young, his face ashen with fear, and he moved like a man going to the gallows. He took the slate from Parmenion's steady hand with his own, which trembled almost uncontrollably, and laid it on the marble altar. There were ninety-six marks upon it now.

Parmenion made his way back down to his palace, his body stiff and his stomach taut with anxiety, but he seemed to his own escort of the Chosen, and to his domestics, as serene a monarch as ever paraded from his temple on a summer dawn.

His hall was chill and shadowed, the hearths cold and the tables and the benches stacked in corners. Tosto stood behind the throne, barely visible, and Zhang Qian, approaching, motioned to his guard to wait at the entrance.

He bowed low before Parmenion, and then raised his eyes and was glad of the men behind him. These barbarian monarchs sometimes were foolish when angered, and the business was a delicate one. The king was old, but old men will struggle hard for their own.

His men, he said in his thin, reedy voice, were encamped some two days' march away, on the river border with a sufficient force. Parmenion stared down at him, and his face might have been graven in ancient stone.

They came in the hope of peace, but prepared for war, Zhang Qian continued. The emperor's need for horses was now pressing. He had borders to protect, and his fortifications, even his great wall, were not enough to keep out the tribes who threatened them. He needed well-mounted cavalry. And there were no horses on earth so fast and so strong as those from the Fergana valley where, he knew, the kings of Sirika had discovered their foundation stock.

The envoy paused. Parmenion sat like an idol indifferent to worship.

Twice before, Zhang Qian went on, he had come to Sirika and had traded mares for the fabulous cloth made only in his master's lands. But the emperor must breed his own horses. He needed colts, and colts had been denied him. This, his august master, the Light of the World, could not countenance.

Here the envoy drew his hands from the wide sleeves of his gown and spread them in a gesture of sorrow. At last, Parmenion spoke.

"Sirika has never been taken."

"My master," the envoy replied, "has never before wished to take it."

Parmenion, grey-faced, grey-eyed and still, seemed not to consider this. In reality his mind raced. His garrison was depleted, but the cavernous cisterns were still full of the winter's rain. From the citizenry he could expect little, and his subservient subjects from the surrounding lands, now gathered outside the walls because of the accursed festival, would turn on their Chosen masters with a vengeance. And what of the regiment that he had sent to the east, to patrol the far border?

From outside the hall, keen in the still morning air, came the sound of wailing voices. The High Priest's body had been recovered, and was being carried up to the temple. Zhang Qian looked at Parmenion with his grape-like eyes, and they were curiously eloquent with what he dared not say. Your god has deserted you, and you cannot prevail.

He went on.

The emperor was a man of peace. He would accept the surrender of Sirika, and Parmenion and his Chosen, and their women and children, would be spared. They might retire to their lands, and pay a moderate tax to an appointed governor each year. Sirika would not be reduced, neither would its citizens be put to the sword. And there was a condition, a matter so insignificant that he would not have mentioned it had not his master been insistent. Parmenion must give up his great stallion.

Zhang Qian tucked his hands into his sleeves, bowed, and waited for a response. To his astonishment he saw that Parmenion's grey face was suddenly mantled with an angry flush.

"The horse is mine," the king growled. "I chose his sire and I chose his dam, and he was raised in my palace stables, to carry me."

"I have come before you," the envoy answered with dignity, "to offer terms for a peace. Not to argue about a horse."

Parmenion's blue-veined hands gripped at the sides of his throne, and his body seemed to twist in anger, but when he spoke, his words came steady and cold.

"If the choice were mine," he said, "I would defy your master, be he never so great. But you come upon Sirika at a time when we make the new king, and I must heed the council."

The envoy bowed.

"I pray, your Majesty, be brief."

Zhang Qian was a brave man, but fear made his back cold with sweat as he made his way, escorted by a squadron of the Chosen as well as by his own men, back down the road to the great gate. Only beneath the stone horses of the great portal did his cramped stomach relax, and with his camp in view he afforded a little smile. The old king was sewing his own shroud, and Sorbon lay in wait to bury him.

Left alone in his hall, Parmenion considered. He had reason now to prorogue the festival and he could continue his reign - until he surrendered to the emperor's overwhelming might.

How he had been blinded! That such an enemy could come to the river border without warning from the tribes! He should have known his weakness, for the Chosen had ever governed by fear, not by consent. The people of the steppe owed no allegiance to the masters of Sirika, the still-strange company of pale-skinned, black-caped horsemen left so long ago by the conqueror. They had watched, and been silent, and given no word to Parmenion's patrols.

The elders of the king's council were easily summoned, most of them from the city place where men congregated. They came, anxious and hard-faced, some embracing their fellows as they met with muttered words of sorrow. Parmenion watched them assemble, giving a nod here and a salute there to men of note. Four of them had been kings in their time, and the old warrior from whom he had taken power was one of them. Once all who could be found were assembled, forty-four of the Chosen stood before their king, and they noted that besides his little mute, the dwarf Tosto, he was attended by that sinister stranger whom all men called the Horseman, standing now in the shadows with his awful familiar. Cephan had visited the mule lines that morning and had led Mule up to the royal stables where the stallion was terrorising the grooms for want of his companion, and during the journey they had been able to talk privately. And while Parmenion awaited the assembly of the council in his chamber, Cephan had told him of Sorbon's plotting.

"How do you know these things?" Parmenion had demanded.

Cephan stared at him, a look that seemed to erase the question.

"How?"

"I listen to what I am told."

"And who is it, who tells you?"

And Cephan had looked that look again.

"I cannot say. But those who speak to me privately, they have no fancies and they cannot lie."

Parmenion had remembered what was said of this strange vagrant, that he had familiars, uncanny ways and secret understandings with his hound and his horses and even that falcon.

"You may trust my words" Cephan had said, and after a long moment, the king had nodded his assent. Then he sent for Cleitus and spoke quietly to him for some moments. Cleitus hurried off and as he went, he eased his dagger in its scabbard.

Now Parmenion ordered the heavy doors of his hall dragged close. The clamour of the city fell away, and the darkness within became even more profound.

The king's voice was as harsh as the sound of iron wheels on a stony road as he recounted to his council the terms offered by the emperor's envoy.

"With the festival already called," one old man said heavily, "should we not wait on a new king?"

"What man," asked another, "would wish for such a crown?"

"The emperor will not wait on our convenience." said a third.

"You see," said Parmenion, "that my son does not attend me. Neither have I called for Antheus, or Bessus. There can be no festival."

Cephan, leaning against the wall and playing absently with the torn ear of the hound couched at his feet, saw how still stood the men below the dais, where a lifetime ago he had come to beg the return of a falcon.

"But the sacrifice! There must be sacrifice! The god demands his due! Why did Cairphas fall to his death? Only in Hippon lies salvation! No mortal power can help us now!"

Parmenion watched the men before him, suddenly seething in terror and despair. Like children calling in the dark for their nurse, he thought sadly. He should have known it would come to this.

For the precedent set by Alexander, in sacrificing his famous horse in honour of the god, had ever after been followed. At the festival's conclusion, the victor rode in triumph through the city to the temple, and there in the courtyard surrendered to the priests the animal to which he owed a kingdom. It was led away into the sacred shades and never seen again.

And indeed, there had been aspirants to the throne of Sirika in the past who, however much they yearned for power, had baulked at this, the price of victory.

Cephan watched from his dark corner. Like the king, he had no trust in gods, not the gods of his birth nor the different deities he had seen worshipped since, called upon in vain in the sack of cities, the agony of death, or on arid desert roads. But like the king also, he knew how men who fastened their hopes of salvation on such phantoms would make sacrifice for their deliverance.

"The priests," Parmenion said, "will ensure that a proper offering is made to the god. They may take what they choose from my stables, or from any of yours."

A white-haired man shook his head.

"We are beaten down by Hippon's anger. He cast his own priest from the temple rock! The sacrifice must be great indeed."

The king glowered at him. That sanctimonious old fool Philotas. But then, how could he know that Cairphas had given his soul for gold and that Parmenion shared the guilt of it.

"Well said, Philotas! Sound words from you once more!"

And they will cost you nothing either, Parmenion thought bitterly, since you keep only mules to ride.

"We shall leave that matter to the priests" he said, "For now, what answer shall I give to this envoy?"

There was a sudden hubbub of voices, some loud and strident, some stubbornly persistent, and Parmenion sat and listened with his eyes moving from face to face, reading fear, defiance, or defeat. But the consensus was clear enough, as he had known it must be. The men of the Chosen ruled lands taken by conquest from the tribes who had been settled there since time began. They were a warrior elite, separate in all things and secure in their citadel. To leave their city, on foot and unarmed, with their women and their children walking behind them, would be to invite the vengeance of those who had suffered under their yoke for so long. And they knew it.

"Retire to our farms! Pay a tribute to the emperor's creature! We should never live to see the day!"

"If we must, let us die like men!"

Parmenion's voice cut out a silence.

"I shall send to the emperor," he said, his words falling like stones in a mill pond, "to defy him. Is there a voice against me?"

"No word from me," said a scarred veteran, "but I am old, and have not many years before me. Should you not, Lord, ask the young men who would rule when you are gone?"

Perdiccas. No better man wore the black cape. Proven in battle and wise. Well respected, as the silence that followed his words made clear.

Parmenion eyed them all grimly for a long moment and then spoke.

"Bessus and Hin-Sho, and Antheus and his father Sorbon, are arrested. They are sent to the place beneath. There has been treachery, and secret dealings with the emperor. They cannot be free while we fight against him."

A silence now so profound that they could all hear once more the wailing, thin and distant, of the mourners for the dead priest. The sound seemed tuned to the slow, incredulous murmur that followed it.

"How can this be?" Perdiccas asked gravely, "for their persons are sacred to Hippon."

Parmenion nodded. He had no fear of rebellion now, for these men had chosen as he had known they would. He spoke deliberately, as if reciting by rote.

"From the day the festival is called, until the victor takes his garland. Unless there is war, famine, pestilence or plague, when the king must break the slate and rule again"

All the men before him in that cold hall knew those words, that time-hallowed rule bequeathed, so it was said, by the conqueror himself. They watched in silence while Parmenion took the slate with its ninety-eight marks and broke it cleanly in half.

"There is war," he said, "and there is more than war. We have an invader who demands our surrender, and we have traitors who have worked secretly against us."

He was addressing Perdiccas, as if others might hear him or not, as they chose. For Perdiccas was revered for a career unstained by ambition. A fine commander and a leader of men, he had never soiled his hands in a fight for power. He would say, and most thought he jested, that he was too fond of his horses to do that. Now he was staring up at the king.

"Is there proof of this, lord?"

"Enough for me, Perdiccas."

"Have they confessed?"

"They will."

Not a man doubted that.

"And so," Perdiccas continued doggedly, "it falls to us to choose the sacrifice. We have denied Hippon his own choice. Ours must be great indeed, for now as never before we are in his hands."

"I say again," Parmenion growled, "That is for the priests."

Perdiccas stared up at his king and almost imperceptibly he shook his head. Other men, watching, muttered among themselves, and Parmenion cursed inwardly.

"It is not for the priests," Perdiccas said, "We must choose for Hippon. The best horse in Sirika."

He looked boldly up at Parmenion, and there was a swelling murmur of support from men who would not have dared to say what all were thinking. Wily old Philotas saw where the wind lay, and he fanned the flame.

"Have no fear!" he cried, "We know our king! He will not flinch from his duty. We sorrow for him in our hearts, that his stallion must die."

The stallion must die. Words of portent so grave that silence fell once more. Parmenion nodded.

"Which priest, which man among you," he asked," will take my stallion to the sacrifice?"

He almost smiled to see their consternation, for tales of Messiah's behaviour had travelled wide, and been embroidered in the telling. It was said that the king's famous horse was fed on the flesh of slaves.

"He will fight all the way to the altar," Parmenion continued harshly, "and kill a priest or two along the way."

"The Horseman might lead him there," Philotas answered, "If he is well paid- - -."

. For the Horseman's fame had spread through Sirika from his first appearance. His magical power over his falcon, his strange empathy with the mighty hound, his familiar, his recovery of a horse which that eluded all other searchers, the spell he had seemed to cast on a stallion that had terrified every groom in the king's stables. And all this before the whispered reports started to come back from the king's farm, courtesy of the picked men of the cavalry escort and others more easily impressed, that the Horseman was a sorcerer who had taught the king's favourite stallion to dance.

Parmenion snarled at him.

"An offering to a god! In grave ceremony! A horse led to the altar by a beggar, a man made filthy and unclean by his life. A vagabond!"

Cephan stood there now beside the throne, as if he had drifted by chance out of the shadows, the dreadful scar on his face tilted to the small light in the hall, seemingly unmoved by the king's words.

"I have no use for your gold," he said.

Then he stepped down from the dais, toward the throng of men who were staring at him as though mesmerised.

There are men who are vulnerable in solitude, who invite long looks and mockery and that sneer that presages the first violence. And there are others, like the Horseman, on whom it seems to cast an inviolable pall, a warning to the world.

Parmenion sat and watched as his council parted to allow Cephan by, and he went unhurriedly, followed by his hound.

Then, without a dissenting voice, the grey mare belonging to Antheus was chosen for the sacrifice. He, after all, was not there to protest. But for Parmenion there were mutinous asides and evil looks. It was whispered, that the Horseman must have bewitched the king's favourite horse, to make him so ungovernable.

And Parmenion knew all these men. He knew the brave and the cowardly, the charlatans and the fools. He knew that his power remained now only until they resolved to take it, and almost tangibly he felt it trickle away like sand between his fingers.

CHAPTER 15

In the dark stone passage, the rush light cast a small, yellow glow and made a long shadow for Cephan, and Khan behind him. The duty guard grounded his spear in salute and then dragged open the heavy timber door of the stable. Inside, a huge heave and a grunt, and a soft nose extending cautiously.

"Well then," the horse said, "what news now? And perhaps to sweeten it, a morsel, a few grains of maize cake made up with honey?"

Cephan had brought this favourite tit-bit for just that very reason. He offered the cake.

"The festival," he said, "is abandoned."

Messiah chewed, head down, exploring the sand for a fallen grain.

"Old news," he replied after a moment, "I heard as much from one of the envoy's horses."

"But I came to tell you -----."

"That they want me for sacrifice? Of course they do, to appease their god, with an army at the gates and the chief priest fallen to his death. But then, if I had carried young

Well Enough to triumph in the contest, what would have become of me then? Strangely, you never told me."

Cephan, standing there, hearing the whisper of the great animal before him in the shadows, bowed his head.

"You forget," Messiah continued quietly, "that I was born here. How could I not know?"

"The king would have saved you."

"And taken their god's own choice? In sight of his own people?"

"Yes," said Cephan, shaking his head in wonderment, "Even so. And I will save you now."

"From what? The stillness? I do not fear the stillness. I am not cursed as men are."

"From your bondage." Cephan answered.

"Remember," the horse replied, "that I came with you to Sirika freely. And that I carry you for my pleasure."

"I told you," said Cephan "when we surrendered to that patrol, out there on the steppe, that I would not forsake you. And I never will."

Messiah turned away. "I told you," he said over his shoulder, "Mule has news for you. He can hardly wait to share the palace gossip. For my own part, I find it tedious."

In the next stall Mule was pulling at his ration of soft straw when Cephan slipped beside him thankfully.

"I have waited for you," Mule said out of the corner of his mouth, "to say what you should do."

"Tell me, O Mule."

"You and the horse, and yonder hound, had best be gone, for the fall of the city is nigh."

"And you?" Cephan asked.

"I am a humble mule, and I carry my load. While I can do so, I am safe enough. A good mule is better than a good horse."

Cephan gave him a pat.

"Thank you. The dice fall quickly now, and there is little time. For the old king and his son have quarrelled, and the prince has fled the city with his lady."

"Truly! Who says so?"

"I have friends in the palace and one particular friend that comes in the night to see me. An old friend. Indeed, I knew his father and his father before him, and I believe his great- grandfather. Khan here frightened him away a little while ago."

"Not I." Khan grunted.

"Do you not recall the old grey rat in the passage? My very own spy. And he lives in the tunnels and the runs behind the walls and beneath the floors of the king's own apartments. And he tells me - - everything."

Mule sighed smugly and pulled again at his straw.

"And what is - - everything?"

"The slave girl has honed the young prince's blade, with a vengeance! For he came to his father to demand that she join the queen's ladies! My old rat was behind the king's armour chest and heard it all."

"When was this?"

"This night just gone. The prince did not want his love housed with the slaves. You may imagine the king's reply."

"He has the cares of his kingdom heavy on him," Cephan replied, "He must have thought himself cursed! To be troubled with a boy's fancy!"

"He thought so too. And he was deep in wine. He threw his goblet at his son and called the guard to have him thrown out. But the lad stood his ground and drew his sword, demanding to be heard!"

"He drew in the presence of the king?"

"He did indeed! And he's lucky not to be in the place beneath along with others less fortunate! But the old king dismissed the guard, saying he could deal with his own whelp if need be, and he gave his son a hearing."

"And what said our young friend then?"

"He said - - that he loved his lady, who was a king's daughter. And that she would be his queen, if ever he came to rule Sirika."

"Small chance of that!"

"As his father told him. Also that the girl had been his until he tired of her. And that, –er—you yourself had had her, along with countless other men, and did he want a queen who was little more than a whore?"

Cephan recalled that pale beauty.

"Never a whore."

"Not for me to say. But the king spoke truth when he said that the girl would never survive the night if she was left at the queen's ladies' mercy. They would poison her out of hand. The rat said so, and he should know. They have been trying to poison him for years."

"Never mind him."

"Save that he tells me this, and I can tell you. The king said, 'You can take her to your bed and use her to your heart's content.' Or that was the gist of it. The rat said he spoke like a common soldier."

"I don't doubt it."

Cephan grinned in the dark.

"The prince would have none of it. Said she must be recognised by the queen."

Mule, who had been speaking freely, pulled once more at his fodder.

"Well?"

"Don't hurry me. The king lost his temper. He said there was no time for such daydreams. That Sirika was in mortal danger. That the city was alive with factions and crammed like a barrel with tribesmen who hated the Chosen. He said that the girl could count herself lucky to be a prince's mistress, and that if she did not like it, he would send her to join the lepers who clean the sewers. Then he called the guard once more, and this time young Mylon was taken away."

"And the girl? What became of her?"

"Sent to sleep with the slaves. But the dwarf came and capered before the king to beg that he should have her."

"Surely he will have supped enough, in the place beneath."

"Aye!" Mule replied, "for the rats down there tell of it. He sucked the blood from men's throats as they died. After they had confessed. But he wants the girl for - - other things."

"Did all confess?""

"All of them save Bessus, who was kept apart by the king's command. But Antheus and his father babbled at the sight of the torture, and Ho-Shin could not suffer long. My friend tells me, the rats of the place beneath were not impressed, considering Ho-Shin was innocent."

Cephan shrugged. His taper was burning low, and Khan was watching in the passage with his head between his paws.

"Not innocent," he said, "but sinful in other ways."

"Indeed. But the dwarf turned the mind of the king against the girl, and he called her a sorceress, and begged that she go to the place beneath. The king ordered that she be taken there to be questioned, but the prince was with her when the guard came, and both have fled the city."

"It seems the young prince had his game well planned."

"Not he!" Mule snorted, "It is the girl who rolls the bones, and she rolls them well."

The little rush light wavered and died. Khan stirred hopefully and was rewarded with a tug of his ear when he stretched and stood up. Cephan grunted a goodnight to the sentry who was half asleep by the stallion's stable, and made his way to his bed.

That night after the curfew horn had sent the tribesmen out to the camps where they lingered, disappointed and disaffected, the great gates of the city were shut against them. Criers under escort announced in the teeming alleys the coming of an army from distant lands, and required townsmen to report for the defence of the walls. And in the dawn that followed, two days before the day called for the now abandoned festival, came the sacrifice to the uncaring god of the beautiful grey mare that had been destined to carry Antheus at the games.

She had been washed so that her coat was like that of a pearly mouse and perfumed, with her hooves oiled and her mane and tail dressed with flowers. She wore a laurel garland round her neck and was led on a white halter between two chanting acolytes into the temple, where the chief priest waited at the altar.

Parmenion, diademed and purple-robed, waited there too, to deliver her with due ceremony to her death. Looking about him, he saw in men's faces solemn faith and the hope of deliverance, and his stomach churned with disgust at what was about to take place and his own impotence to stop it.

At least the brute will know nothing, he thought. They would have given her the poppies in her maize, the mixture that Cairphas prepared so skilfully. Enough to make her quiet, to drop her neck obediently to the gentle tug of the halter and accept the falling axe on her poll but still alert enough to walk that last walk without staggering.

He came to lead her forward, the offering of a king to a divine god, reciting the long- hallowed words, beseeching the deity to accept their humble gift and to grant them relief from their mortal trials. He saw before him Cairphas's young successor, waiting at the altar with the great bronze axe, trying to conceal his trepidation with a look of calm sanctity.

This will be his first time, thought Parmenion. At that moment he felt the halter rope tighten in his hand, and saw from the corner of his eye that the mare was standing with her head erect and her nostrils flaring. She gave a snort of alarm and stepped backwards. He held her, with the white-robed acolytes on either side, and knew with sick certainty that the priests had failed with their potion.

But they mastered her and made her still, and she yielded unwillingly to the downward pull on both sides of her nose.

"Quickly now!" Parmenion muttered.

But the mare, already nervous, saw the falling axe and twisted her head away. The blade chopped into the big vein in her throat as she dragged at the rope, and in the next moment she was on her hind legs, towering above them in terror with her forefeet flailing and blood gouting from her neck. Parmenion, blinded by the sudden red cascade, was yanked from his feet as she swung away toward the open archway behind her. The black-cloaked Chosen in her path, come as witnesses to a solemn sacrifice, scattered before her like frightened crows in what was now a scene from a charnel house, but she slipped on the entry steps and crashed down into the dawn light where, gathered in the court, the men of the city waited to pay their humble homage, to join in this, the offering by the Chosen to their god.

What they saw instead was the frantic butchery of a terrified animal, her grey coat splashed with her own blood, kicking out in her last agony at the swords that struck into her, screaming in panic until a haphazard thrust chopped open her windpipe. When the business was done, and men stood back mired by the red filth of it, some with their black cloaks sodden with scarlet, the mare lay twitching in her own blood, which ran down the temple steps in a spreading pool.

There was a complete silence. In the archway Parmenion looked down at the ghastly gang now standing back from their work as though they might disown it. Beyond them, he saw faces riven by fear, anger and despair. The sullen faces of men who had looked to him for intercession with the god, and had been betrayed. And the king knew then that Sirika would fall.

But kings cannot give way to doubt before their subjects. Parmenion came down into the court with his escort and the crowd gave way, but there were muttered curses from either side. Fools, he thought bitterly. *They will say I have angered Hippon,, that I should have sacrificed the stallion. What children they are, slaves to their beliefs! Never will they think that it was the fault of the priests, that the mare was not doped, that the new boy with the axe lost his nerve. For them, Nippon has refused his offering and will punish all of us.*

CHAPTER 16

The king's physician, with an ear over his patient's heaving chest, listened intently. Then he moved his spindle fingers like spiders over Cephan's body, naked but for a loin cloth. His eyes were closed, and his occasional mutterings were the only sound in the dark, narrow cell. There was a fragrant stink of herbs burning on the tiny charcoal brazier, and by the curtain entry waited a slave with a water bowl. Khan watched the old man from a corner, lying bloated with a belly full of horse liver. The choice parts of the grey mare's carcass had been sent to the royal kennels, with the remainder to the slave kitchen. It was evening, and all day Cephan had kept his pallet.

"Well," said Parmenion, "will he live?"

He had been overseeing preparations for the defence of the city since daybreak, and he was tired, but he had come to see for himself. He stared down grimly over the bent shoulders of the physician who turned now to face him, folding his skeletal fingers together as he bowed low.

"The man has lived near death, Lord. He is hard made and carries no flesh. But he breathes out his own blood, and no mortal can do that and live to be an old man."

Parmenion nodded.

"Can you aid him?"

"Indeed, lord, for I have studied my healing craft in the fabled lands in the east, and have sat at the feet of the most renowned doctors there. Also - - -."

" Can you aid him?" the king said again.

The physician drew himself up.

"I can give him a longer span if he keeps his bed and is well nursed. Or I can ease his pain, and give him back his strength, but with potions and drugs so powerful that his life will burn away more quickly still."

The king nodded.

"Leave us. Very soon there will be work enough for you."

Parmenion, alone now with his horseman, seemed to soften. The lines of his face were not so deep, and his eyes lost their grey, unflinching stare. His shoulders fell slightly as he looked down at Cephan, prone on his sweat-stained pallet.

"Could you take the stallion back" he asked abruptly, "to the place where you found him?"

"Ridden by the king's horseman, who would not lead him to the sacrifice? I should be stoned from the gates, and then your men would turn on you!"

"There is no place for him here," Parmenion muttered, "A city under siege. I have ten days' forage and then - - - there will be mouths to be fed. And mine must be first to the slaughter. And how long, we do not know----."

His voice trailed off, and then he thought to comfort his horseman, who might have been his friend if he, Parmenion, had not been a king.

"I shall see you yet," he said, "in that little house, in the shade of that vine that bears a good grape. We shall sit there together in the evening."

Cephan smiled the shadow of a smile.

The king stood for a moment by the bed, looking down, seeming to find his departure difficult. Then words came, harsh and reluctant words.

"I wished for a son like you."

There was a faint cough of mirth from the mattress.

"If wishes were horses, the beggars would ride."

When the king had gone, and Cephan had supped water from the bowl, Khan raised his head.

"The king weakens." he said.

Cephan shook his head disbelievingly.

" He knows that Sirika will fall and that he will perish. And yet he schemes to keep our friend the stallion safe, dreams that I might spirit him away!"

"He might think more of his kingdom! Messiah cares not for him!"

"Nay, Khan," Cephan replied, "he cannot care. Not even for me. He is a horse, and it is not in his soul to care for men, as it is in yours."

Khan lay quietly on the floor beside his master, considering this.

Cephan pulled his nearest ear.

"What do you know, Khan, of this emperor?"

"What I am told."

"By?"

"By Messiah, who has it from the envoy's horses. If you could just scratch behind the other ear - - -."

"And what did he tell you?"

"The emperor is old and very fat. He comes night and morning to see his horses, and he is pushed in a small cart, for he cannot walk. He calls them by their names and gives them bread from his hand. They say he knows all their names, though he cannot name all his women."

"Are they many?"

"Very many, both horses and women. The horses told Messiah that all are as beautiful as they are - - -. Thank you. That was pleasure indeed."

"They made a fine show, those blacks of the envoy's escort. And the women?"

"He calls them his pearls, picked from his own seas, and all are flawless."

Cephan turned on one elbow, the effort making him gasp.

"Must it be you alone that rides Messiah?" asked Khan.

And suddenly Cephan recalled the words of his father's old horse master, in another world long ago.

"Truly, the gods have honoured you with a great gift. In your hands and in your mind there is a feeling for any horse you will ever ride, which will be like a charm upon the beast. I can teach you nothing more, and there is now but one counsel left for me to give, and it is this: receive with humility what you have been given. Do not be proud. Remember that the grace and the glory belong to the horse."

And the old man had twirled his grey moustaches, and had embraced the youth whom Cephan could only dimly identify now, and there had been tears in his eyes.

Now, in the little chamber, his whisper was loud in the quietness.

"Yes," he said, "why it should be I cannot tell, but the stallion will bridle only to my hand and listen only to my voice."

Khan stirred uneasily in the almost-dark.

"And when the time comes, Master? What then for us? Will the king save us also?"

A gasp of mirth from the pallet.

"We are but trifles, Khan, thou and I!"

Silence once more. Then, from outside the door, soft steps and a cautious entry by the old physician.

"Drink."

Cephan drained the proffered bowl. The liquid was hot and bitter, but he lay back with a strange sense of ease and the strength to speak what was in his heart. The old man left without another word, and Cephan began.

"It seems, Khan, O my shadow, that we come to the end at last - - -."

The great hound whined and thrust his nose at the bed once more.

"I smell no fear of the stillness." he said.

"I am not afraid," Cephan replied quietly, caressing the heavy head in his lap, "The stillness must come to all, lest the earth be burdened with the sadness and the grief of old men, and there be no magic land for youth and love and laughter, such as we had long ago."

"My memories are different indeed."

"Well. But hark. When the stillness comes, I shall be gone from you - - -."

"Not so! For my life is yours, and yours is mine, and we travel together always."

Cephan sighed.

"Yes, to the way's end! But then must come a parting. Lie down, Khan."

For Khan could not comprehend death, even though death had been a familiar all his violent life. He had seen death fall savagely or suddenly on man and beast alike. But the stillness was for all creation except him, and this was his god gift and his curse alike.

Cleitus, once more at his station above the great archway, had seen the horizon shift shape and colour all day. Beyond the grey-green wasteland of the steppe, fractured only by the trail that led to the gate beneath him, he had watched first the small black mark between land and sky, and then, as it grew larger and longer, he had made out the divisions of an army on the march. The setting sun was glinting now on innumerable spears and on armour, and he could see the dust of cavalry as men deployed to either side of the road to make camp.

His eye travelled down to the nearer plain beneath the walls of the city, to the wells and the road where it crossed the amphitheatre, and to the rocky slopes below Sirika. A full day since the gates had been shut against the tribesmen and the traders, the warning cried among them that an enemy advanced on the city. And yet, there they were still, farther from the walls indeed but not gone. Not alarmed and not surprised. Waiting, Cleitus thought, for something better than a festival. They must have known of the dead-slow movement of an army across the steppe that was their home, as must the merchants and the vagrants who travelled the road. And yet this army had moved behind a mighty silence, and Sirika was now its prey.

Cleitus scratched his beard, then took off his bronze helmet to wipe the sweat from his face. They sowed their seed, he thought, but they did not first till the earth and let it settle. They came with their famous conqueror, with their horses and their pride, and they ruled by the sword and were hated for it. And now the reaper comes, and here am I, with them but never of them, called again to the battle.

He shook his head, thinking of the Chosen, under whose banners he had served - how long was it now? – Certainly the best part of his life. He had been – how many summers old? - when he had fought with the young Parmenion, and saved his neck in that frontier ambush. Strange men, all of them, with the black capes of their fellowship, their horse-god, and their one hundred founders of Sirika. That was all piss in the sand, of course. There were Chosen men now whose fore-fathers had been camel drivers. The curious thing was that they were the men who held most dear the ways of the elect. Perhaps not so surprising, if he thought about it. They had all paid handsomely for their privileges, if half he had heard was true.

The sun was down now, with a last red-rag flourish to herald the cold night, and in the dark distance twinkled the sudden light of innumerable camp fires. Cleitus stamped off on his round of inspection, and found his men alert and watchful. As well they might be, he reflected grimly as he returned to his own post directly above the archway.

For there would be blood spilled before long and a greater game to be seen by the watchers below. Cleitus could make out in the shadows the still forms of baggage animals standing to their tethers. Too many, he thought, on land scraped bare and with the wells near to exhaustion.

He searched the horizon once more, measuring distance with a soldier's eye. Parmenion had made his dispositions, and on the whole Cleitus approved them. Defence of the city walls with mercenaries deployed, and then retreat to the never-taken fortress, garrisoned now by the remaining Chosen regiment and the old warriors who had sought sanctuary there with their kindred.

Women and children, girls and boys, sons and daughters. All would have a hard time of it if Sirika fell. Cleitus, who had seen rape and murder enough in the sack of cities and settlements, shrugged. Never take a wife, and don't own the children had been his principle. That way a man fought for himself with a clear mind and regretted only his own fate. Not like that poor sod who had once been a young soldier and was now a king, broken with care and deserted by his own son because of a slave girl.

And to cap it all, Parmenion had ordered Bessus brought up from the place beneath, where his rivals for the kingdom had all died under torture, and good riddance, and hailed him as a long-lost comrade! Much to the annoyance of that little fiend, Tosto, who, not content with the blood of the others while they died, wanted to fix his teeth into that throat as well.

Cleitus had heard all this from his drinking companion, one Haidan, who was duty guard in the place and had been glad to bring a man up from the darkness and the screams and to stand forgotten at the door to Parmenion's chamber and, dumbfounded, be witness to the meeting. For Haidan was an old soldier, lamed by a Tartar arrow, and he had that ability, so useful to a soldier when volunteers are being sought, to become part of the scenery.

Bessus, having been well fed and watered in a kennel by his horsedealer master Hin-Sho, had almost come back from the dead, Haidan had said, sitting in the wine shop by the gate the previous evening. He was a man again, and they had cleaned him up, and he had embraced Parmenion, and there had been tears, yes, tears in the old king's eyes.

His innocence was apparently accepted with another embrace. Never, Parmenion had cried, would he have believed himself betrayed by the dearest friend of his boyhood.

"Ah!" Cleitus had said while the Etruscan girl they both fancied poured the wine, "There's the bottom of it! And talking of bottoms - - ."

He had smacked the girl's buttocks, and she had landed a blow on his ear that had made his head ring. He remembered it now, still at his station above the gate, scanning the night and the pale road below.

As he had explained to Haidan, playing the elder statesman in his cups, that was why Bessus had lived and the others had died. Same breed, you see. Same blood, traced right back to the beginning. He and Parmenion had swaggered side by side in the palace, had ridden together on the training ground, had had their girls together. Until Bessus had lost his banner and been disgraced, they had been insepar - -, insep (hic) -- together all the time.

So that even now, with that eastern bastard at the gates, the king remembered his own.

Haidan had cast his eye about the wine-shop shadows, but the place was quiet, and he leaned forward over his bowl,

"How long?"

Cleitus had shrugged, just as he shrugged now, standing there above the gate and watching those fires. He remembered his answer, that only a kind god could help Parmenion now, and how Haidan had laughed bitterly.

"Small chance of that then, when he keeps the stallion for himself and gives Hippon second best! Small wonder the god refused the mare!"

But Cleitus had been a cavalryman all his service and was suddenly saddened.

"She was no small sacrifice." he replied.

And there had been the scornful reply,

"Stolen from a traitor? If Antheus was a traitor, which I for one don't believe - - -. And unclean, the priests would say if the king had not their tongues!"

At that Cleitus had sobered up.

"He'll have yours if you let it wag like that!"

And Haidan was a good man, Cleitus thought, looking up at the heavens and tracing the patterns in the stars. If such as he turned against the king, then surely the sky would fall on Sirika.

For all men the time comes, he reflected, and his hand strayed to the small ivory god that he carried on a thong around his neck. Not a great god like Hippon, but then he was no great man. In this coming battle watch over me, he prayed, as the stars twinkled above.

They still do, of course, but they are not visible to the naked eye because of the red glow that is now a constant on the horizon that Cleitus watched so carefully long ago. The camp fires of an army have been replaced by the electric wasteland of the city at night, and you can see how the motorway, or what remains of it after constant air strikes, snakes toward the World Heritage site of Sirika, following more or less where the ancient trail wound through the steppe, now a tired old counterpane of different crops mostly left to rot because of the war.

Cleitus's small talisman was for many years on display in the city museum, once a renowned safe haven for beautiful and ancient things. After it was blown up by the followers of a more recent deity, presumably at his divine behest, the little repository of one man's prayers was sold to a private collector in New York to support the family of a suicide bomber. We will not trouble you with the details, for they are no part of our tale.

CHAPTER 17

News travelled fast to the king's stables, with the constant to and fro of grooms and messengers and horses being led out. Abdullah in a fret now, looking over his maize and his straw, trying to calculate rations for his charges once the city came under siege. Cephan looked into Mule's stall and found him quietly chewing his fodder. He came about, though, to poke his long nose at his visitor.

"There is a smell on you." he said, "Curious - - -."

He paused, and sniffed again.

"Poppies. How strange."

"It is because of a remedy I have drunk," Cephan replied, "My breath stinks of it, but it makes me strong again."

Mule's soft, grey muzzle moved gently against Cephan's chest.

"No remedy that, I think," he muttered as he turned away to pull at his straw.

From the next stable Messiah snorted impatiently, and Khan was already beside the barrier with the sentry waiting to pull it aside, but Cephan lingered with his old friend.

Mule was a more restful companion than the stallion, for a proud horse can be very tiresome. And as he always said, a good mule is better than a good horse.

"Well," Mule said with his mouth full, "short commons now, I suppose. Until those who carry the rations become the rations."

It was one of the well-worn, bitter sayings of the baggage train.

"Better off in the king's stables than on the picket line." Cephan answered.

"I am in my proper place," Mule said gravely, "beside Messiah. As it was foretold, so it has come to pass."

"You are there, O Mule," replied Cephan, "because I arranged it so. Not Destiny. Me."

"You are but the instrument of fate," Mule replied compassionately.

Cephan moved on.

The sentry grounded his spear in salute and dragged aside the barrier. Messiah loomed like a monument, his red-gold skin aglow in the half light. Khan settled in a corner on the fresh sand, shoving away the boy whose place it had been, who fled hastily with his basket. Truly I never saw the like of him, nor ever will again, Cephan thought. He stepped to the horse's shoulder and laid a caressing hand on the high arch of his neck. Abdullah's boys have done him well, he thought, seeing how the silk mane fell through his fingers.

"Yonder mule," he said, "is your disciple."

Messiah's massive head came round, the nostrils puthering at Cephan's body.

"Poppies. And yes, when a prophecy is fulfilled, then come the disciples."

"Are you then - - -?"

"A god? As I once told you, men make their gods. And so do the creatures of the baggage train. Once there is a prophecy, it needs only a messiah. Prayers and priests do the rest.

"And you - - are you such a one?"

"Since I was dropped in these very stables, it seems. Set apart by the king and cherished for my might and my beauty. I learned the prophecy with my mother's milk, as all do. And as chance would have it, I was born in a palace. Men took me, and I went free to the mountains. I fled all who came after me, enjoying my freedom and my mares. But I did not flee from you, and so by chance I came in from the steppe. As the prophecy foretells."

They stood now, the man and the horse, so close. That strange closeness that horsemen know, that is so secret. The great chestnut head with its white blaze like a light in the darkness, lowered to the man in front of him.

"And yet, O Messiah, for all your greatness, you offer nothing. You cannot ease the suffering of the baggage train where the prophecy was born."

"What do the gods offer? When they slaughtered the grey mare, did those priests truly expect mercy from their almighty Hippon? If you believe that, you can kiss my backside!" Messiah swung away, suddenly morose.

"Well then - - -."

"A messiah offers hope. Prophets proclaim his coming, and for long years the people wait. But then the time comes, and lo! The messiah has been found. He takes the mantle and embroiders the plain stuff of it with a few gold threads of his own. What else can he do, when men look to him for their salvation? And being mortal, he goes the way of flesh, but he leaves behind a hope that comforts them as if they were children in the dark, and so he is a deity still."

"And you, O Messiah? What do you offer?"

"Not the promise of another life, believe me! For we who bear men and their burdens, we the iron-shod kindred of the road and the battle, we do not fear the stillness. We are truly afraid only to - - ."

Cephan's hand was gentle on the horse's neck.

"Be alone." he finished.

"Yes. Not the lonely road of the day's work. But the empty stable, the deserted paddock, the friendless barn. We were born to mind our fellows, and find comfort with them. We cannot be content alone. Even I, Messiah, must have my lowly mule beside me!"

Cephan glanced aside, where Mule with his long ears was no doubt listening in his stall.

"A good mule," he said, "is better than a good horse."

"So you keep saying," Messiah replied crossly, "though I can't think why."

"Forgive me. You were saying - - - ."

"Only the thoughts of a horse who is not as good as a mule."

Cephan thought, he can be sulky when he likes. He reminds me of Phaedra.

"The prophesy is," he said, "that after the messiah has come, there will be an end to the sufferings of the trail brethren and that men will rule them no more, nor take them to the battle."

"I know not what follows me. But the messiah of the baggage train brings hope, like the messiahs of men."

"Hope of what?"

"Hope of the day's end, the burden lifted. Hope of water and good forage and never a lonely stall. And our most cherished hope. Freedom. Freedom to wander forever with our own kind beneath the skies."

"And what becomes of such a messiah? Cephan asked, standing there, and for some reason he bowed his head.

"Have you not come to tell me? You must tell me my fate, for I am in your hands."

"I do not know it. Men come from far away to take the horses of Sirika. They will lay siege to the city, and if the siege is long, there will be no place for horses."

Save in the shambles. He had seen it before, cavalry horses slaughtered for meat.

"And you said that you would not forsake me!" the stallion said sourly.

"Nor will I. Until the stillness comes upon me."

Messiah's nose was soft and warm on Cephan's neck.

"You have said so," he replied with indifference, "and I hear your words."

He nosed at Cephan again.

"It will not be long."

"No."

Going to his bed that night, Cephan crossed the garden court and paused by the pool, suddenly aware of an absence behind him. Khan. He looked about in the bright moonlight and saw nothing. Then he looked up beyond the court to the white stone temple, and there, looking out over the plain below, he saw his familiar, seeming to watch the moon. And as Cephan stared, he saw the great hound tilt back his head, his ragged ears flat on his skull, and begin his cry.

And this is the song of Khan, which he gave out to that moon and those stars so long ago. I set it out here, as best I can recall it, in case you should think it has some bearing on this history.

"I, Khan the mighty, the undefeated, slayer of wolves, find in my soul the fate of all things, and so I prophesy!

The quick-eyed people, the children of the dog-saved, the clever-fingered folk, will rule the earth and all that is in it, even to the great waters and all things that abide there. They will multiply like the locusts, and like the locusts they will leave nothing save the desert. To all the creatures of the earth they will bring death and suffering, and from those under their tyranny they will exact toil without mercy. They will bring such wars as will destroy the plains and the forests and burn up the seas with mighty fires, and at the last they will destroy themselves.

"And I, Khan, curse them with a great curse. That in time they will reap their harvest, and eat the fruit of it, and with full bellies go famished to their coward graves. That they will drain from the earth foul waters and strange soils, and crust the fertile land with the filth of them. That they will find ease and idleness, and having no purpose for their bodies, they will yearn for more. That being full grown, they will want the things of childhood and play the games of boys. And that their fear of the stillness, which is the black seed in them all, will grow strong in their failing hearts, and that their long-forsaken gods will not heed their prayers.

"So that we, the broken and the disinherited, we who tread the earth lightly, we who drink but do not foul the waters, we who have suffered the workings of these devils incarnate through the ages, might at last be avenged!"

The long, wavering howl rose up to the stars and drifted over the plain beneath them. And in the moonlight, as Cephan watched, he saw far below him a great, quiet stirring, as if ghosts were hunting shadows through the camps of the nomads. The couched camels, the mules and the asses in their pickets, all raised their heads as if they listened to that eerie song. Some got up, pulling uneasily on their head ropes, and from the tents dark figures came to quieten their animals. There was a sudden flare of fire where a hearth was disturbed, followed by a shouted curse.

And when it was over and the night silence fell once more, Khan was gone into the temple shadows, and a few moments later thrust his muzzle into his master's waiting hand.

Dawn over Sirika, and in the king's stables Abdullah once more fussing like a old hen along the passages. That his charges had had an uneasy night he could tell from a glance at their disturbed litters, and now they were snatching hastily at their feed and standing with heads erect and listening ears, forgetful of hunger. And yet for the moment there was nothing amiss. The city awoke quietly enough, with no alarms from the walls and no clamour in the narrow alleys. More quietly than usual, indeed, with men grave and silent, all mindful of their peril, of the host suddenly at the gates. But the horses were restless, whether because they sensed the battle or for some other reason Abdullah could not tell. But he was too much a horseman to ignore the signs, and to relieve his anxiety he lashed out with his stick at a passing lad as he went to look over the most precious of his charges.

Messiah stood patiently enough, chewing his morning maize with the honey stirred in, and moistened as he liked it. He permitted two slaves to strop vigorously at his already burnished hide, while a third stood on a stool to plait his mane into long braids and a fourth teased out the knots in his silken banner tail. But from time to time he too stopped feeding and went to the barrier with ears pricked and head raised, as if waiting. Then he would return to his maize, and the boys resumed their work at his pleasure.

The guard, awaiting his relief, confided in Abdullah.

"He was down in the night, as usual, until he heard something that had him up on his feet in a trice. There was a wolf howled, but nothing out of the way. And they were all up, every nag in the stable, and they none of them went down again. They know there's something in the wind, if you ask me."

"I do not ask you!" Abdullah snapped.

Fitting, perhaps, that on the sand of the arena swept ready for the games should take place this other meeting, this other contest between players in a greater struggle. A private meeting in that two small bands rode together to the centre of the space, with their escorts waiting some distance behind. But public also, seen from the walls of Sirika and witnessed by the huddles of curious tribesmen and merchants who had come for a contest of a different kind that very day and now waited silently on the stone terraces as Parmenion met the emperor's envoy once more.

Zhang Qian's spy had come to him in the night to whisper that the tyrant king had had Sorbon and his son arrested, though he could only guess the reason, and so the conspiracy for the swift reduction of Sirika was aborted. He would have to lay siege to the city or turn for the journey home with his captured horses and his men baulked of their prize. The horses were now corralled by the river, some hundreds of them, and he knew only the fittest would survive the long march. And in not so many moons, winter would fall across the steppe and snow would block the passes. Yet if only he could take with him the golden stallion, all might yet be well for him, for the Light of the World would scarcely notice that the distant fortress of this barbarian had not been reduced.

Then fortune's wheel had turned again, this time to favour him! For in the very early dawn there had been brought to his tent two heavily cloaked captives taken as they blundered into one of his outposts. The king's son, no less, and a girl with him!

For indeed, Mylon, knowing what would befall his love at the hands of the dwarf, had fled with her to the royal stables and taken horses. At the North Gate he had been lucky, for Cleitus was not on duty, and the stripling who took his place that night dared not challenge the prince and ordered the gates opened. But then Mylon's luck had changed, and as he made for the wells to seek a friendly caravan, he had been captured. His fine clothes, the accoutrements of his horse, the girl with him, all gave away his ill-thought lies.

And so Zhang Qian, disappointed by his spy with the news of Sorbon's fate, had hours later that same night listened to the son of the barbarian king, with a girl standing silent and empty-faced beside him. And Mylon, loudly proclaiming his love for her, had told - the truth! And had demanded the envoy's protection in good style, as became a prince and a man in love.

Zhang Qian had gazed at Mylon with his black-olive eyes and had wondered if he himself, in his far-off youthful folly, might ever have behaved so, and had rejected the very idea.

"Keep them confined, and separate" he had ordered abruptly in his thin, reedy voice "but treat them well. For now."

Mylon had struggled as he was taken away, but the girl had simply lifted her heavy veil and had looked after him with, the envoy had been fascinated to discern, the faintest of smiles, before she went quietly with two women of the camp.

And now Zhang Qian, sitting on a fine bay horse this morning with his escort behind him, told the king of his son's capture, as dispassionately as a gambler letting fall an ace on the table. As Parmenion listened, apparently unmoved, his gaze moved from the man before him to the escort behind, to the array of warriors, rank upon rank of them in the distance.

The envoy's thin voice ceased. The terms he offered were unchanged. Mylon would remain his guest.

Then Parmenion's grey gaze fastened on him like a blow in the face.

"We the Chosen," he said, "have never surrendered. No king of Sirika may do so now."

The place of that meeting, on the plain below the citadel, where Alexander rode his famous horse, where all the contests for the crown of Sirika were held, was the obvious choice for a car park in the years when the tourists came in their huge, air - conditioned coaches and struggled up the slope to the iconic ruins of the gateway. Now there are only the burnt-out wrecks of a Russian tank and a Toyota pick-up. The ticket kiosk has been a convenient latrine, and the large poster that displayed the scale of charges in nine languages is now a sieve of bullet holes neatly traced by a Kalashnikov-toting freedom fighter, to make a point that might seem obscure to the rest of us.

There had been bitter fighting at the gate, where the Chosen, under Parmenion himself, held off the enemy. Cleitus fought bravely, and we know that here died the commander of the patrol that had escorted Cephan into Sirika with the stallion. He had not then trusted the mercenaries at his back, and had time enough to know he had been right, left to fight alone with his back to the wall in one of the alleys he had been detailed to defend. But the Chosen were battle-hardened men and were fighting for their lives, and their vigorous counter-attack had sent Zhang Qian's troops in retreat back to their camp. He heard of the repulse from his captains, and he gave a deep sigh.

A barbarian kingdom ruled by that uncouth warlord, in a wilderness peopled by hostile tribes. And fate had led him here, years ago, to find horses for his master. If only he had failed! If only he had returned empty-handed! If only he had not, on his knees before the Light of all the World, reported that he had found the fleet steeds of the Fergana valley and then, travelling farther in the unknown lands to the west (such was his devotion to his duty, poor servant though he

211

was), that he had arrived at the court of King Parmenion, where he had seen such horses as men ride only in their dreams. And a colt, a young stallion that might have been made for a god, so splendid a creature was he.

Fool that he was! A clever man like him, a seasoned diplomat, left babbling on his knees with his eyes carefully fixed on the yellow silk slippers in front of him! Could he not have guessed the response?

Surely not so great as the imperial horses!

Zhang Qian had hesitated. A mere moment of irresolution but fatal, nonetheless. He had heard the swish of the emperor's gown, and when he dared to look up, the divan was empty. He received his orders the following day. He was to return to the king of Sirika once more for breeding stock. And he was to bring back the colt, the horse that might have been made for a god.

Remembering this, Zhang Qian eyed the steep crag of the citadel. His men had lost many scaling ladders in the retreat, and he had no siege engines. He had gathered the harvest he came for. And if he attacked the fortress, he would face desperate resistance from those strange, black-caped warriors. And all because he had not held his tongue!

Surely there was a better way.

Another meeting under flag of truce. Parmenion confronted Zhang Qian, on the bay horse once again, and the envoy took care to speak very clearly, so that the king's escort could hear every word.

"I will hold my hand from your city," he said. "Your son I will return to you, and for him I will take the golden horse."

Parmenion sat silent on his horse for so long that the envoy despaired, but then came the response, uttered like a curse.

"He is no son of mine."

Zhang Qian had a thin, reedy voice, but it carried well enough to the men behind the king.

"Then he must die."

The envoy had been sure of the outcome. Of course a father must save his own son. But then Zhang Qian looked again into that doomed visage, saw the awful, manic, cold eyes that gazed on him as if they saw the gates of Hell, and with horrified amazement knew the reply before it came.

"So be it."

Parmenion spurred his horse, and rode back to his city. As he dismounted in the courtyard of the citadel, he saw how the captain of his escort looked at him and then, deliberately, away. It was a swarthy youth whose name the king could not recall, but he remembered now that the lad was Hephaestion's lover.

Cephan was in his chamber when the king's physician came.

He felt his patient's pulse with a dirty claw, put his ear to Cephan's chest, and shook his head.

" I am strong," Cephan smiled, "like a young man again. Your mixtures have made me well!"

"There will be a price," the physician replied. "As I foretold you. According to your own choice."

"How long now?"

The old man had answered many such questions in his time.

"The gods decide."

"Shall I know the time?"

"You will hear the pounding of your heart, and your breath will fail you."

Cephan nodded.

"Thank you for your wisdom."

The old man turned, and hobbled sadly to the women's quarters where one of the queen's maids needed help to calm her hysterics. The queen herself, he had been told, was demanding potions of quite a different kind.

Cephan lay with his eyes closed. There might be little time now, he thought, and perhaps no rest after all in the shade of that little dwelling with its own vine, bearing a good grape, with his hound, grey-muzzled now, at his feet. Instead the dark, with Khan left to mourn him, and to die in his turn.

As to more secret thoughts, his serene face, his limp, resting body, gave nothing away. He was a man cloaked in privacy when first we met him at the gates of Sirika, and he remains so now as we near the end of our tale. We have learned but little of him, and that little not much to his credit. It happens sometimes that a foolish woman is intrigued by a man simply because he does not disclose himself. She thinks there might be a diamond hidden, and does not see that there is nothing to discover. Perhaps Cephan was such an empty shell, and his soubriquet, the Horseman, told all there was to be said.

So, if he was afraid of death, or if he welcomed release from his suffering, we shall not know it.

If he reflected now, as his time approached, on a violent, sinful life ill-spent, we could not guess it from his tranquil repose. If he recalled now, as some men will as they near that gate we must all pass through, the days of his childhood or a girl's embrace, there was no trace of such feeling in that scarred face turned now to the great hound by his side.

He was resting by the lily pool when there came a rush of pinions, a swooping rise to the parapet, and a hovering descent to the polished stone where long talons scrabbled for a purchase.

"So," said Phaedra, folding her wings and cocking her head at the man below her, "you live on."

"As do you," Khan said with lifted lip, "until my master comes to his right mind, and wrings your neck for you."

Cephan held out his fist, and she settled there on one leg, with a wary eye on the hound.

"I had thought you carrion ere now."

"And so I would be," Cephan replied with a wan smile, "but the king requires me, and so keeps me alive."

"For why? But let me guess! He needs you to keep his sacred stallion safe."

Cephan nodded.

"Poor old king! With the enemy at his very gates, he fears for his horse!"

"Indeed. All judgment is gone."

"No matter," Phaedra said, "with such an army to overthrow him. And what becomes of his precious stallion then?"

"May the gods attend him" Cephan muttered.

She roused her feathers importantly.

"I, Phaedra, the all-seeing, know what awaits him."

Cephan waited. The falcon blinked at him coldly then explored the talons of one foot with her hooked beak. Khan yawned. At last she went on.

"There is a pen ready for your precious stallion. I spied it in the dawn light below my wings! And there the tartars wait, to bleed him until he paddles in his own blood and can scarcely stand. And then they will scourge him so that he cries like a child - - - Did you ever see a horse beaten so?"

Cephan shook his head, but he was trying to dislodge a memory, not to hear the screaming. So many years, and so many sounds of pain and terror had melded in his mind. But not that memory.

"Did you not? Your face tells me differently. But they know how your stallion may be defeated, those tartars. The irons lie by the charcoal in readiness, for they will have him so weak he will stand to be branded like a new-born calf!"

"And what could they do with him then?" Cephan asked bleakly.

The falcon on his fist eyed him malevolently.

"You know the tartars! How they manage their horses! You who have drifted away your life on the steppe, you know them! And what they will do to your stallion!"

" An emperor does not play with broken toys, Phaedra."

She cawed triumphantly.

"He will have life enough to seed his mares!"

Suddenly, Cephan was conscious of the beating of his heart. He drew a deep, painful breath.

"If he is broken so, he will not last the march. And if he did, he would never cover a mare again."

"You may tell the emperor so!"

She lifted her wings again, rising on his fist before the morning sky, her deathly beauty an image taken out of time.

"Farewell, sweet Phaedra!" Cephan said bitterly.

The lethal head swivelled downward, the cold eyes scanned about, the last words framed.

"Your time runs out" she said, and in a moment was gone, lifting on the down-sweep of her wings.

Later that day, and drowsy because of the physician's potions, Cephan was roused by commotion on the city walls. From his vantage point where he overlooked the North gate far below, he saw that men were staring out across the distant plain where the envoy's army was encamped.

A cart drawn by a span of white oxen was being drawn slowly toward the great gate. As it neared and then halted beyond bowshot, they could see that on its flat bed stood a figure naked but for a loincloth and bound to a sturdy post, his hands lashed behind it.

Zhang Qian was responding to the challenge of the barbarian king on this very day when his power ran out. It was the one hundredth day, the day of the festival when the Hippon chose a successor.

At that time, China was a country where the methods of capital execution were strangulation and beheading. The first was considered the more merciful because it left the body intact for its own spirit, but that was not why Zhang Qian had chosen it.

It is a death which may be swift if the executioner knows his work, but it may also be done by degrees, as the envoy had ordered. Not because he was a cruel man. Simply he expected the stallion to be surrendered by the father to save the son.

As men gazed grimly from the walls of Sirika, two figures robed in black, like a pair of crows, busied themselves

217

about their captive on the plain beneath. The day was bright, but the men above the gate, and Cephan from his vantage point, could not make out what was being done. But there were tribes people out there who could see more clearly and suddenly a woman cried out.

The advent of death can strip us even of humanity itself. We recoil, trembling, our eyes dilated to take in those last moments of the light. We piss ourselves in our fear, and we sob for reprieve. And so it was that the prince's thin, pitiful appeals reached the distant city walls while hardened warriors swore and women screamed. There was no wind to cleanse the air of those final prayers for mercy, and the memory of them, I believe, seeped into the heedless great stones of Sirika and remains there still.

But Parmenion stood above the great North gate, silent and unflinching. He had heard the screams of tortured men in the place below, had seen the defeated beg for mercy on the field of battle, and beheld death so many times and in so many forms. And this man, choking now as the silken cord befitting a prince tightened round his throat, had never been in his heart a son, always the prompt of sad misgiving and scorn. The king remembered even now that last exchange between them, with Mylon screaming like a thwarted girl when he was taken away by the guard, and his face cracked in contempt. And so he waited there until suddenly the victim's head lolled forward, his body twitched for a moment and then was quiet and still. There came then a profound silence, from the watchers on the city walls, the tribes people on the plain below, the army drawn up behind the envoy.

Zhang Qian, sitting on his horse some little way in front of his own camp, watching for any sign of submission from the gate of Sirika, shook his head in disbelief as he turned away.

Finally, the body was cast into the dust and the cart returned whence it came, followed by shouted curses from some of the watchers on the city walls. Men shrank from the king as he made his way to his palace with his escort stony-faced about him, commanded still by Hephaestion's lover.

For posterity, we can record that Zhang Qian had permitted the young man a last meeting with his love. That it was the last meeting Mylon well knew, for when the envoy had softly explained to him what was to be done and what was hoped, the prince, ashen faced, had shaken his head.

"You will fail," he had wept, "for that cursed horse has taken my father's mind."

None of this disturbed his lady. She had slept well that night, being destined as well she knew, for the envoy's bed.

It is a great matter to kill a king, even one so broken. The leader of the conspirators was Hypphaestion, and Pediccas was there, doing what he conceived to be his duty, though some of the men behind him were there to settle scores of their own. The sentry at Parmenion's door stood aside, affecting not to see the drawn blades, but the king had heard the footfalls in the passage, and had time to reach for his sword as the assassins burst in. The struggle was short and bloody, and Parmenion defended himself alone save for Julia, the old wolfhound bitch who laid down her life for her master, being his faithful comrade to the end. Tosto gibbered like an ape and dodged the vengeful blades in the shadows until another frantic blow nearly severed his head. When it was over, heavy- faced and breathing hard, the conspirators left the bodies where they lay and went to wash their hands among the lilies in the limpid pool in the king's garden. Then, with unhopeful eyes, they turned to each other. With an enemy at their gates, they had murdered their mad king. Who was to lead them now?

At dawn all of the Chosen who had spoken for the death of the king, and some who had not but saw the way the wind blew, attended upon the priests and found the hallowed precincts of the temple forbidden them. Regicides, the chief priest explained, with the blood of a king fresh upon their hands, could not seek the mercy of Hippon in his sacred place.

Hyphaestion stood forward.

"We have not killed a king," he said, "We acted to remove one who usurped the throne. His reign had run its lawful course. We seek only to placate the god, and to know how we must behave to do so."

The chief priest, he who had bungled the execution of the grey mare, returned to the shadows of the temple and prostrated himself before the altar for some time. The black-caped Chosen shifted uneasily. Finally, he returned.

"There is a horse that is cursed" he proclaimed "a horse that assailed the mind of the king. While he remains in the city, Sirika cannot rest. Let him be sent out to your enemy."

For a priest, if he does not direct events, must know when to progress them usefully.

There was a murmur of assent, cut off by Hephaestion's clear, confident young voice.

"We the Chosen" he said "will abide by the will of Hippon. Does he desire that we surrender the city, or that we fight to defend her?"

"The stones of Sirika," the priest replied, "will stand forever."

Later that morning, under a truce, the envoy's dead were recovered from beneath the city walls, and a squadron of the Chosen under Hephaestion took back the body of Mylon from the dust where it lay. The queen had begged for the corpse, but Hephaestion forbade her, saying rightly that it was no sight for a woman. Told of the death of her husband, she had turned away with a curse in her own native tongue.

It was Hephaestion too, who under that same flag, met the envoy. He sat so proudly on his horse, spoke so clearly, had the squadron at his back so ably controlled, that Zhang Qian smiled inwardly. Strange, he reflected, how a crisis can throw up a king.

King Parmenion, made distraught by his son's execution, had retired to his palace and left the defence of his kingdom to his able captains, said Hephaestion. Zhang Qian smiled inwardly once more and simply nodded.

Would the envoy accept the golden stallion as a gift, together with gold to please his men, as sufficient reward for so long a journey? Had he not already taken very many of the Ferghana horses for his master?

"Well," replied Zhang Qian, "Then show me this horse."

Hyphaestion had been much occupied that morning. His mind unsettled by the enormity of what had been done, he had worked to secure the city, to set guards at the palace and to strengthen the resolve of his fellows. He had simply not expected this workaday response.

"There is no need, Excellency," he replied, "This is no common steed. Already he is a legend!"

Zhang Qian smiled openly now.

"I am past the age," he answered, "when a man buys a horse he has not seen."

And he called out to his escort behind him, something which made them grin. Hyphaestion swallowed.

"Your Excellency must give me a little time - - -."

Zhang Qian shook his head.

"Time is costly. The sun is already high, and my captains are impatient. I will not wait upon the delivery of a horse."

Hyphaestion swallowed again

"I will have him ridden out before you. If you will retire a while, the horns will tell you when he comes. You will not repent the time taken, Excellency."

Cephan had heard the turmoil in the dark, the sudden quiet, and then later, the sobbing of Nooran the chamberlain, wailing the news of the king's murder all about the palace. He had stepped warily out into the precincts, and had seen sentries posted at all the gates. He knew that he was hated, that now his life hung in the balance, that he was unprotected. His escape already impossible, he had retreated to his chamber, where his dagger was tucked under the pallet on the floor.

And now hurried steps in the passage, Khan afoot with gaping jaws, and the door flung open.

Nooran, with his robe comically awry to show his flaccid stomach and his face streaked with tears. And behind him, thrusting him aside, Hyphaestion with other grim men in support.

"Come with us! You must ride the stallion."

Hyphaestion was breathless and sweating hard, having raced all the way up to the palace. And Cephan, standing behind Khan who was straining at his collar, saw suddenly that he might for some time at least be safe.

"And if I will not?"

The young man glared at him, awful threats rising to his lips, his chest heaving.

"You must ride him! The envoy waits to take him as tribute, and the fate of Sirika depends upon it!"

Cephan looked curiously at his visitor and his companions, all at once in his power.

"Peace, Khan! Lie down!"

He seemed to consider.

"And for me?" he said quietly, at last.

Hyphaestion took a deep breath.

"What do you want?"

"Safe conduct from Sirika when the horse is taken and the enemy gone. And to be treated gently, for you see I am not strong. I need some time to ready myself."

And he smiled ruefully.

"I am old, and unarmed, as you see. I will trust to your mercy, and I will obey you, if you grant me a little time. Abdullah has to prepare the horse fittingly, you must remember."

Hyphaestion glowered with impatience. He had forgotten that. He turned to one of his men and gave an order, and the man hastened away.

"Come as soon as you may. I shall leave a guard, for your own safety."

"I am grateful," Cephan bowed, "I shall look upon him as a friend."

Hyphaestion turned to go.

"And one more thing."

"Yes?"

"I am no longer the guest of a king. I must have my price for my work."

"There! Fine gold for a fine rider!"

He dropped the heavy coin on the pallet and hurried away.

The sentry, a nervous lad, took his position in the passage. Cephan smiled at him apologetically as he shut the door in his face.

"We are safe," he murmured, "until I have delivered up Messiah. Then they will kill me, and you, Khan. We must spin out our time."

It was later, much later, than Hyphaestion had wanted. The sun was slipping down the western sky when Cephan slipped into Mule's stall, with Messiah snorting in bad temper close by.

"My!" Mule said when Cephan slipped into his stall, "What a fine fellow, to be sure!"

Cephan smiled, the lop-sidedness less noticeable now that his beard was closely trimmed, as was the greying hair of his head, giving the effect of a hatchet blade newly burnished.

"But still a friend to a good mule!"

"And a good mule - - - ?"

"Is better than a good horse!"

Khan lay down in a corner with a weary sigh.

"And the hound also!" the mule exclaimed, sniffing gently.

The hound snapped at his grey muzzle bad-temperedly.

"So," Mule continued, hastily retreating, "it seems there comes an end at last. Is the prophecy to be made out?"

"Ask the soothsayers or the priests, O Mule, not a humble horseman. But you shall know, by the setting of this sun."

Mule shifted uncomfortably.

"And the Messiah?"

"His fate awaits him."

"Then I must follow, and bear witness."

Cephan patted the old mule's dusty neck.

"Be content," he replied, "for you shall indeed."

Then he nodded to Abdullah, who was waiting, and Abdullah cried out.

"Bring forth the horse!"

There were gasps of admiration as Messiah stepped proudly from his stable. His skin, the tresses of his mane, the banner of his tail, all rippled like molten gold, and he stepped upon the stone flags as though they cushioned his oiled hooves and set them springing. Dwarfing the slave to each side of him, he waited upon Cephan's inspection, softly champing his bronze bit so that the white saliva dribbled from his mouth, with his ears flicking nervously and his eye following his rider, who now stood back from him and studied every detail of his appearance, checked the girths and the fit of the saddle, then stood back again for one last, unhurried, searching look.

Then he gave a satisfied nod, and mounted. Dressed all in black, he seemed to the men who watched him to be set apart, high above them on the great stallion's back. It was as if he had joined another world, as if he and the horse belonged together, and had been always waiting for this moment.

CHAPTER 18

Behind the gates, Messiah stood surrounded by a throng of men. Abdullah, close to tears, wiped a fleck of foam from his shoulder. Cephan, immobile in the saddle, could feel the steady throb of his heart, his deep, even breathing, the mighty horse beneath him gathering the muscles of his back in readiness. Before him rose the golden crest of the stallion's neck, the braided fall of his mane, the ears now widening as they flicked back to hear his voice.

Then Hyphaestion gave the order, the horns sang defiance from the ramparts, and the gates flew wide.

The land still lies now much as it did then. The ruins of the amphitheatre have been neglected for lack of government funding since the recent war began, but the road that leads from the city and runs across it follows more or less the same track that Cephan rode that day more than two millennia ago. And the sun sets over the same horizon, falling more swiftly to the earth beneath as the evening comes.

Of the envoy's forces, as they stood to arms at his command that day, there is only mortal dust and the twisted scraps of bronze thrown up by the plough. Nothing, not a wisp in the wind, to conjure for the mind's eye the ranks of infantry, their swords and spears, the archers waiting with bows unstrung, the cavalry aloof, all parading in their barbarian splendour before their lord.

And if there can be less than nothing, no trace either of the men who watched from the slopes above the amphitheatre, the nomads and the desert dwellers, the steppe folk and the itinerant merchants, the soothsayers and mountebanks and jugglers, all assembled there for games of a different kind, and waiting now to see a greater spectacle on this, the day after the one hundredth day. Thin, frugal, stick-like beings, inhabitants of nowhere and owners of nothing but their tents, their women and children, and their lean, hungry beasts. An insubstantial gathering, easily blown away by wind and time, so that you might picnic there now, if you can suffer the almost magical appearance of the beggars, and never guess at the host that came before you.

And so Messiah bore his burden before them all, a great, golden horse carrying his rider down onto that sunlit arena.

Cephan and the stallion beneath him bewitched by their own harmony, the horse moving with the reins lying loose on his blood-gold neck, toying with the bit in his foaming mouth, as if he trifled with his own shadow and cared not to trample it. All eyes followed him as he responded to shouts of applause as a great flame is fanned by the wind and seems to race and leap above the earth where it is born.

And then, as Cephan rode Messiah in stately parade along the ranks of the tribes people all standing in a disorderly line, there ventured out a small boy, leading a kid goat on a rope. Cephan saw him first, still some distance ahead. He had time to bring the stallion, apparently obedient to his rider's hand, to a quiet halt. Cephan saw the horse's ears flick forward, heard the snort of alarm, and felt underneath him the massive lift of his back.

"Gently!" he said, through his teeth, "It cannot hurt you!"

But Messiah was turning already in his own length, setting his jaw ominously, uncaring now of restraint, and Cephan could only turn with him and ride back, passing off the revolt as a spectacle to be cheered. As it was, at least from the envoy's pavilion beyond the pillars that marked the boundary of the arena. And while Zhang Qian at last understood why his master had sent him so far, there came to Cephan a sudden thought, a thought that became the answer to a prayer.

And then he halted with a final parade before the entourage of the envoy, and Messiah stood as still as bronze, alert and looking beyond the confines of the amphitheatre, beyond the crowds of men and their beasts, and he neighed an arrogant shout and seemed to listen for a reply.

In the years that followed, it was a boast that guaranteed a man a hearing by the nomad's fire, or in the hall of some stone fastness when the wine cups were filled, that he had been there to see King Parmenion's stallion that day. It chanced sometimes that a listener would put forward the claim of another animal to such glorious fame, and give the narrator the chance to dismiss such spurious nonsense with a partisan version of the truth. In this way, the golden stallion passed into legend, and in the centuries that followed, in lands where children's tales and history were told in song and poetry together, he found the power of flight and became both a guardian and an avenger of the weak and the wronged. On stormy nights, from the mountains to the deserts and across the steppe, mothers would quiet their frightened children, telling them that the tempest was but the king's golden stallion galloping on the winds.

But then came times when such stories were not needed. In a concrete apartment block a child does not fear the weather, scarcely knows whether it rains or shines. And mothers come home from work too tired to tell tales to their offspring, whom they picked up from the day nursery only an hour ago. And anyway, the little people seem to be so happy with their computers. How clever they are! Adults before they can walk, not to be deceived by fairy tales! And so time filters history, and a small particle of gold passes through the sieve unnoticed. Almost. For I came across a collection of old Arab tales in an antiquarian bookshop in Istanbul only last year, and there, when I came to translate the ancient script, I found a story of a golden horse that belonged to a king of long ago who set him free rather than see him fall into the hands of a conqueror. But that, I think, is the only remaining echo of the events that I chronicle here.

Returning behind the great gates, Messiah humped his back and lashed out with a hind foot. He was sweating, and the blood ran close to his skin and seemed to redden his golden hide. His eye rolled white, and his ears flicked constantly, back and forth.

Cephan slipped from the saddle and Hyphaestion, forgetful of his cares, seeing the deliverance of Sirika within his grasp even at so great a cost, looked at the tired horseman with grudging admiration.

"I never saw such a horse" he said, "Pity indeed that he goes now to the emperor."

"Forgive me, Sir" Cephan replied, "It is late. The night comes fast. I cannot take him to a strange camp now. I am not strong enough, if he takes fright in the dark. You must send to the envoy, to say I will bring him at first light."

Hyphaestion groaned in frustration, and the men about him muttered.

"Come, Sir," said Cephan "you know, never to make haste with a horse."

And so it was agreed, and Cephan went back to his chamber with his youthful guard.

"You must protect us well," he said anxiously, at the door, "Me and my old, toothless hound. For you see, I have no weapon."

The lad grounded his spear and took up a position.

"I saw you ride that horse," he replied, "It is an honour to stand at your door."

A while later, when the cries and calls in the beleaguered palace seemed to diminish, he was pleased to come to Cephan's faint call from the pallet in the dark chamber. Water? Of course he would fetch more water. He did not wonder why that hound was so still. He propped his spear against the door and leaned over the recumbent figure to take the pitcher. And took the wet thump of Cephan's dagger in his chest. And then again, to be sure.

It was a sad death, however necessary, for he had been a promising young fellow. His mother was one of the queen's own ladies, and she had loved him dearly.

In the king's stables there was no order now. Both sentries in the passage dozed on their feet, and in the stalls the litter was dirty. In that dead time of the night, when the cold strikes hard in still, slow moments, came Cephan once more to the stallion, who gave a soft snort of disbelief.

"I never thought to see you again, who betrayed me! Young prince Well-Enough is dead, and his death is to my charge, it seems!"

"Because you cannot answer for yourself. Men favour such a one when comes the judgment."

"Ah! The dog-saved folk! They will give me to the envoy to spare their mad king and say that I am cursed, not he."

"They have not spared him." Cephan replied.

"But they will surrender me!"

"They are frightened men, afraid for their lives and for their women and children. They say their god has forsaken them, that he rejected their offering because they did not sacrifice you, and because the king schemed to rule again through his son and pervert Hippon's own choice. They say Parmenion bribed the chief priest, who cast himself in despair from the temple rock. And they say you have so ruled the king's mind that he saw his own son murdered rather than lose you."

Cephan gave the horse a thoughtful pat.

"Perhaps they are right." he added.

"Right or wrong, I must suffer for their folly" Messiah snorted.

"I came to bid you farewell, and to counsel you" murmured Cephan.

"You swore you would not forsake me!"

"It will be best, if you do as I ask of you. First, do not let them take off this halter, a new one I have made with magical stitches - - -. There, it becomes you very well."

The great chestnut head came down, and Cephan slipped it over his ears. It was a simple rope halter, but finely made for a treasured animal, white rope bound with soft leather where it sat over the horse's poll, to prevent chafing there.

"Good. Very good. You are a good, brave horse. All will be well."

"You say so. You who betrayed me!"

"Second, you must go quietly with these men. Probably they will come on foot, so that their own horses do not anger you, and they will lead you away. Men of Sirika, or the envoy's men, I do not know. They will lead you down the road, across the space where you carried me so well lately - - -."

Here, an approving stroke of the long white blaze.

"And through the pillars that mark the end of the arena. If you go quietly, all will be well."

"That I should trust you now!"

"I do not ask your trust" Cephan said.

"And you?" the horse asked, "Shall you be there to see what befalls me?"

"I shall be there. You will not see me, but I will be there."

"And shall I see you again?"

"Never."

A last caress, a long stroke of that shining neck, and Cephan was gone with Khan behind in the darkness. In the passages of the palace armed men hurried, and there was shouting, and once a woman screamed. In the street that led down to the North gate confusion and smoking torches, and a convoy of laden mules heading for the open archway where Cleitus still held his command. The envoy was impatient for his gold.

Cephan might have passed out with the baggage train in the shadows, but for the huge presence at his heels.

"So," said Cleitus, "Time to leave Sirika now!"

Cephan silently held out his palm, and Cleitus saw the glimpse of gold. He shook his head.

"I will take nothing from you," he said, "for you are cursed. Go!"

And he gestured to his men, who stood aside.

"Cursed or no," said Cephan, "I thank you."

"I spare you only for the old king's sake" replied Cleitus, turning away, "He would have wished it so."

Cephan stepped out into the dark, beyond the unsteady torches and the press of men and mules, and made his way to the tents of the nomads, where they waited to see what would befall the city of the Chosen when day came. He was in search of a goat.

At dawn, the envoy came to look over his tribute, the part price of his forbearance. The chests of treasure were not so many as he had expected, nor their contents as great. Certainly his men had searched the king's vaults for themselves, but the envoy thought they might have come too late, that a large part of that fabled hoard might already have been hidden away. Angry and impatient, he hardly contained himself when the messenger came from the city, to say that it would be best if the envoy's own men came for the stallion, for his own grooms had fled.

They came, six of them, to the stables. Squat, silent tartars, nervous and afraid. Concerned to see that Messiah was fit to cover mares, that he was undamaged either by accident or by design, one of the men crouched by his belly.

"Bigger than yours!" yelled a voice from the passage. The stallion kicked out, and the tartar took a glancing kick in the face that sent him staggering. Someone hooted in mirth, and Messiah plunged against his halter ropes. But the tartars were tough, and went stoically about the business. It took some time, with the horse becoming more recalcitrant and the stable folk jeering at their efforts.

Finally, the stallion, with three men on either side just sufficient to contain him, was led down the narrow way that led to the great gate. Beyond lay the envoy's distant pavilion. Excited by the sight of open land, Messiah plunged nervously. There were catcalls and jeers as the gates were drawn shut behind him, until Hephaestion angrily called for silence.

He was dog-tired, but he was lifted by hope. All that was wanted now was the safe passage to the enemy of this cursed horse, the last of the tribute. Sirika would be safe, and he the saviour would be king, to renew the power of the Chosen once more. He glanced about him, at the faces of men who had been his friends and were now somehow set apart. Faces drawn close by secret thoughts as they all looked down from the rampart above the gate.

The tartars struggled with their charge, but slowly he was taken down the road, a captive now where he had moved like a golden god, and came to the pillars that marked the ending of the arena and the beginning of the dusty highway.

And then, suddenly, he planted himself, a monument as intractable as a stone. The tartars struggled vainly on their ropes, and one produced a whip. The horse reared with a scream of fury that could be heard on the ramparts. Clouds of dust rose around him as the men fought helplessly to control their charge and he pulled them like dolls from side to side in a panicked fight for freedom. Six proved too many, for they fell over each other in the struggle. And Messiah was a stallion who had fought for his mares and fought to keep them, and he knew the power of his driving hooves and the use of his savage teeth. It was hard to see what happened in the confusion, but then the stallion reared again, high above his tormentors. And it seemed that the rope halter was torn apart, for it fell away, and suddenly the horse was free.

There came a long gasp of astonishment from the watchers assembled there, from the ramparts of Sirika, the tents of the waiting envoy, and the slopes above the road where men had stood to see the king's famed horse taken away to a new captivity.

For a surprised moment Messiah stood like a mighty, new-made bronze, his skin red and wet with sweat, uncertain now. He neighed once again his arrogant shout, but this time he seemed to hear an answer. And to his eagerly distended nostrils there came the heavy scent of the far steppe and the distant snows, and soon he was gone to the plains and the hills, and to another freedom.

Cephan, having tethered his stolen goat to the pillar as the day dawned, had climbed back up the hillside and found a rock for shelter, where he huddled in his long coat with Khan to warm him at his side. They did not wait long to see Messiah led out of Sirika, to witness the sudden, dusty turmoil, his fight for freedom. And they heard his triumphant call, and saw him go.

We shall not meet them again, this strange, inseparable pair. Cephan seems a little stronger now, for how long we cannot say, and Khan's terrible life has weakened him, but there was still the hope of that last resting place, with a vine for shade that bore a good grape. They came from the night at the beginning of this history, and into the night let them return, down the same road.

CHAPTER 19

Z hang Qian studied the broken halter that was brought to him, and saw that the rope had been cut where it would have passed over the horse's poll and held in place merely by the soft leather binding there. He ordered the six unfortunate tartars to be shackled together so that they could be marched back to face the emperor's displeasure, and wondered why that young upstart should have been so foolish. Perhaps the horse was cursed indeed, he thought, and brought madness to all who dealt with him.

Now his army must have the sack of the city, and he would be a fool to deny them. Further, he was now desperately short of supplies and he knew that Sirika's stocks had not yet been depleted by siege. His captains had readied their men to march that morning, and if he acted swiftly he would have the advantage of surprise.

Hephaestion saw that in the morning sun the envoy's host seemed to shake itself like a great dog, and then the ranks advanced upon the city. Cleitus had the gates dragged together, and his guard went to their posts. The Chosen were now alone in their defence of the city. Many of the people thought them doomed, with their king murdered and the chief priest dead by suicide, and now they had seen from the walls the flight of the fabled horse whose surrender to the enemy was to bring reprieve. Truly the Chosen were damned, and their power gone. Not before time, men said to each other as they hid their small treasures and barred their doors, and left their erstwhile rulers to defend the walls.

The Chosen could not hold the ramparts of the city against the determined attack of the envoy's men. They were hardened campaigners, lithe as cats, and they came up the walls in their hundreds, calling out in high voices like children in school while from behind them crossbowmen fired their quarrels at defenders silhouetted against the pallid sky. In the fierce fighting below the North Gate Cleitus was severely wounded. Dragged to shelter by his friend Haidan, he looked down at the gaping tear in his stomach and weakly grimaced, and with his eyes dimming, he fumbled for his talisman and gave it to his friend. Haidan's fate we do not know.

Hephaestion rallied his companions as they retreated to the Palace of the Winds in good order, some of them choosing to stand and fight to cover the men who dragged shut the doors behind them. One of these was Bessus, happy to be shield to shield with his brethren at long last, and to die with them and so redeem himself.

There was some respite then while the enemy brought up their huge, bronze-headed rams. The old queen, sceptre-faced and firm, offered the poison to each of her ladies in turn. One of these was the mother of the lad murdered by Cephan, and so she was spared the grief of his loss. All swallowed the draught save one young girl who could not confront the moment, and the old queen embraced her with a sad blessing before she too raised the goblet to her lips.

When the doors were broken down, the first rank of the Chosen stood before their enemy, and as each man fell another came up to fight in his place, until the final, savage onslaught.

One of the last to die was Hephaestion, who had bravely commanded the last remnants of the Chosen in a defeat which, like Custer's Last Stand, might have endured in history as a great victory if it had been remembered. Hepheastion himself, we know, was a gifted young soldier with a life of fame and glory before him, save that the gods decreed otherwise, and cut him down to be forgotten with his fellows.

In the time that was left to them, the priests dragged into place the great marble slabs that closed the entrance to the sanctuary behind the altar. There they were slaughtered in turn, their throats cut in a last, almost ritual sacrifice to the angry god who had so forsaken them.

Their bodies, like all the rest, were stripped and thrown into the city's wells and the cisterns before the invaders departed, their stinking, bloated corpses left to foul the water for years to come.

The sack of the city lasted throughout the day which following the assault. The invaders, in their quilted jackets and conical helmets, swarmed and seethed in the streets and the alleys like hungry bees and raped and murdered at will. Zhang Quan had ordered that there were to be no prisoners, not because he was a cruel man but because he knew there would be no rations and no guards available for the journey home. Some of the prettiest boys were spared, however, after they had been castrated, as was the queen's young handmaid who had chosen life rather than poison.

The envoy had the chests of gold and silver from the king's treasury drawn before a parade of his exhausted troops. It would be divided fairly among them, his captains shouted, on their safe return with the horses for which they had come so far.

On the night before that long march began, Zhang Qian came from a troublesome meeting with his quartermasters to his tent, to find Phoebe there as he had required. Already he had discovered how completely she was protected by her own compliance, how her beautiful body was hardly worth the taking once his lust was slaked. But he was an intelligent man, and he thought that if he could but touch her mind, then he might have a treasure indeed. And so he had been kind, and had told her how she must return with him to a far country where a great emperor ruled, and perhaps be taken into his court.

Now, sipping his tea before a brazier, for the night was cold, he told her how the Chosen had been slain and their fortress taken and how on the morrow he would begin to retrace his steps back through the Ferghana valley and travel east into a far greater kingdom.

"And the horseman?" she asked in her fractured voice "What became of the horseman?"

Zhang Qian frowned, not understanding.

"The horseman" she persisted, "he who rode the golden stallion that is lost. Who had with him always a great hound, and a falcon that came sometimes to him. What became of him?"

Now the envoy remembered the frail, black figure who had so effortlessly controlled the might of that accursed animal.

"I do not know," he said, "in the fall of a city, one man among so many - - -."

The girl had not shed a tear for Mylon, had no concern for the fate of the queen's ladies, had not mentioned another soul from her captivity.

"What was he to you?" he asked her gently.

Phoebe smiled, with secrets hidden in her eyes.

"Nothing" she replied.

As we know, Sirika stands there to this day, a World Heritage site and a marvel of the ancient world. For Zhang Qian left the House of the Winds to the nomads and the steppe people, and the city was left to stand deserted, visited only by goatherds, vagrants, and storms. The story of its final days and the mad king who sacrificed his son to save a horse was told for many years, and finally passed into legend.

In this modern age, where the past is so much more appealing than what we can see of our future, the House of the Winds, the temple, and the palace, have all been extensively surveyed by archaeologists and learned men, and there has been much speculation as to the origins of Sirika. None of it accurate, for the Chosen were but an afterthought of a great conqueror, who survived longer and better than might have been expected. They came as strangers to the land, and as strangers they remained. They left no written word, no songs and no chronicles, and for a century or so the steppe people would look toward the rock that dominated the plain and mutter a curse. And then the

Chosen were forgotten.

It may be that in days to come, clever men with modern instruments will discover the hidden entrance to the sanctuary that lies undisturbed beneath the ruins of the temple. If they do they will find evidence that might lead them to the truth. But we, being merely the teller of this tale, cannot assist them.

As all conquerors learn, the spoils of victory must be carried away, and mules and oxen and camels must be rounded up and dragooned into service. And so it was that our friend Mule found himself once more on the road, heavily loaded with provisions and with a harness that pressed hard on his withers and made them sore.

Toward the end of a long day's march, down a rocky mountain pass, he went lame and was flogged unmercifully down to the arid valley where the convoy was off-loaded. Often he fell to his knees, which became gashed and bloody, and was beaten again until he staggered to his feet. He was lame on that same foreleg that had let him down on the journey with the horseman back to Sirika, but this time there was no one to help him. The back tendon was hopelessly ruptured, the leg swollen and hot and the skin as tight as a drumhead.

After the laden panniers had been lifted from his back, he was given a little, a very little brackish water and tethered at the end of the picket rope, and an overseer came to inspect his injury. Then he was moved a further distance, so he could not reach for the ration of poor straw that was strewn before his fellows. Mule knew what this meant, as did they, and he was left to his solitude, the loneliness of the condemned.

He knew they would not dispatch him now lest the violence of it and the smell of blood, disturb the other animals and make them less tractable. He knew, too, that come first light, when the camp stirred, he would see his load portioned among the rest while he was left unharnessed. When the camp was struck, and the order for march given, the mule train would file away, and men would come to him where he stood alone, looking after them. One of them would carry the pole-axe and another a few grains to persuade him to lower his head. His body would be left for the foxes and the vultures.

And yet Mule was strangely content. He knew that he had borne his last burden, that he would suffer no more. That he played his part in the coming of the golden Messiah, and lived to see how he too carried his burden, the strange rider for whom he danced before them all. Now he would go to the eternal pastures where the grass was tall under a benign heaven, and the wind was kind, and the streams ran cold and clear with water sweet from distant hills.

In the still time before the dawn Mule waited patiently, until the light broke open the eastern sky.